Zimbolicious 10th Anniversary:
New and Collected Non-Fictions

Edited by Tendai Rinos Mwanaka

Mwanaka Media and Publishing Pvt Ltd,
Chitungwiza Zimbabwe
⚹
Creativity, Wisdom and Beauty

Publisher: *Mmap*
Mwanaka Media and Publishing Pvt Ltd
24 Svosve Road, Zengeza 1
Chitungwiza Zimbabwe
mwanaka@yahoo.com
mwanaka13@gmail.com
www.africanbookscollective.com/publishers/mwanaka-media-and-publishing
https://facebook.com/MwanakaMediaAndPublishing/

Distributed in and outside N. America by African Books Collective
orders@africanbookscollective.com
www.africanbookscollective.com

ISBN: 978-1-77928-205-7
EAN: 9781779282057

DISCLAIMER
All views expressed in this publication are those of the author and do
not necessarily reflect the views of *Mmap*.

TABLE OF CONTENTS

3

About Editor

Tendai Rinos Mwanaka is a multidisciplinary artist, writer, musician, editor, publisher and producer with over 70 individual books and curated anthologies published in US, Northern Ireland, UK, Cameroon and Zimbabwe. He has 5 music albums, with new album, *For Mberikwazvo: The Winter After* (2025) recently released and his music is playing in at least 18 radio stations in US, Canada, UK, France, Israel, Brazil and Australia. He has hundreds of paintings and drawings, thousands of photographs, some exhibited, published and sold. His pieces have appeared in over 500 journals in over 35 countries and his books and writing is translated into at least 11 languages. His music can be licensed here: https://www.songtradr.com/tendai.mwanaka. And find him here: https://m.facebook.com/tendai.mwanaka

Contributor's Bio Notes

Tinashe Muchuri is an author, field researcher, actor and a storyteller. He has over ten published fictional titles which are studied in the local education system. He is an expert in field work and that has taken him to Binga, Hwange, Chipinge, Bindura, Chivi and others, gathering and recording people's stories on various social issues. He holds degrees in Media and Creative Writing. He is an award winning media writer in creative cultural industries. He has an interest in Social history, Human rights, and the indigenous knowledge systems. He has been invited to give presentations, stage performances in poetry and storytelling and readings in Zimbabwe and abroad.

Jabulani Mzinyathi born on 01 September 1965 is a poet / novelist. He has several published poetry collection and a chiShona experimental novel. He is an avid reader too. Jabulani is a reggae fan who is greatly influenced by Peter Tosh, his favourite artiste. Jabulani is a former teacher, ex Magistrate and is currently is a lawyer in private practice based at Beitbridge , Zimbabwe .He is a human capital manager and is also a change management practitioner. He vows to keep on reading writing.

Tanaka Chidora is a literary scholar with a PhD in Literature from the University of the Free State in South Africa (2018). He taught at the University of Zimbabwe in the Department of English from 2014 to May, 2021 before joining Goethe University as a Humboldt postdoctoral fellow researching on violence, memory and literature in Zimbabwe. Additionally, Chidora is a published poet and short story writer whose first poetry collection, *Because Sadness is Beautiful?* (2019) was published in Zimbabwe by Mwanaka Media and Publishing.

Dr Tembi Charles is a poet and writer who grew up in colonial Rhodesia and because of her family's involvement in politics she experienced first-hand the struggle for black freedom. Dr Charles' poetry and stories captured this period and its aftermath

Benniah Munengwa is a poet and reviewer for one of the major Zimbabwean newspapers, *The Daily News*

Zvikomborero Kapuya is the author of Phenomenology of Decolonizing The University: Contemporary Thoughts in Afrikology

Killian Nhamo Mwanaka is a Zimbabwean former freedom fighter, soldier, journalist at *The Vanguard 1984*, Editor of *Gweru Times* 1988 –1992; stays in London, is a businessman, was published in the seminal anthology of Zimbabwean poets *Now The Poets Speak* and lately in *Zimbolicious poetry anthology, Vol 2*

Bute Martha Chipo is an avid reader, a powerful prose writer, an enthusiastic poet and a correspondent to a regional church magazine. She prides in expressing thoughts, feelings and social matters through writing. As an English Secondary School teacher she aspires to see a youth of the 21st century stand in difference through writing as she nurtures the skills to them.

Nkosiyazi Kan Kanjiri is a Zimbabwean poet, writer, and social worker whose work bridges literature, and social justice. Born in Harare to a Ndebele mother and Shona father, his multicultural upbringing informs his nuanced exploration of identity and resilience. A 2024 National Arts Merit Awards (NAMA) nominee for his poetry collection *Looking for Mother (2023)*, Kanjiri's evocative verse, featured in anthologies like *Best "New" African Poets (2018), Eagle on Iroko (2016) and Zimbolicious: An Anthology of Zimbabwean Literature and Arts Volume 3 (2017)* , captures themes of love, loss, and resilience. He co-authored *New Diversity Dawns*, a ZIMSEC O-Level Literature set book published by Zimbabwe Publishing House, shaping the educational landscape for Zimbabwean students. He earned a Bachelor of Social Work (Cum Laude) at the University of Fort Hare, South Africa, on a 2015 scholarship. Currently, he pursues a Postgraduate Diploma in Social Work at the University of the West of England (UWE Bristol), residing in Bodmin, Cornwall, UK.

Preface

10 years ago we started on the Zimbolicious Journey by issuing out *Zimbolicious Anthology Vol 1*, which was an anthology of Zimbabwean poets. The Vol 2 was still a focus on Zimbabwean poets, but in the third volume we expanded it to embrace other Zimbabwean arts and literature, e.g. drawings, paintings, essays, short stories etc.., and ever since this anthology series has been publishing all these until the last we issued, Vol 9. So we have decided this year to look back and ahead this journey by issuing out anniversary anthologies. Because in the fifth volume we focussed on an anniversary centred on the genre we started with, poetry, we have decided the 10th year anniversary should focus on prose (fiction and Nonfiction), thus we created two anniversary anthologies. One for fiction, one for nonfiction. We collected some of the essays and stories and added a few new ones from contributors of these anthologies

This one, *Zimbolicious 10th Anniversary Anthology: New and Collected Non-Fictions* has 26 Non-fiction pieces. Killian Mwanaka starts the anthology with his newest three part searing nonfiction piece on the war of liberation and how the government has used and abandoned the war veterans. Tendai Mwanaka drives the anthology forward with a total of 6 nonfiction pieces on Zimbabwe's politics, death, inspiration and an experimental look at the poetry call. Others like Munengwa, Muchuri, and Chidora cut their teeth on literature and literary traditions of Zimbabwe. We have pieces to do with the mismanagement of Zimbabwe, interviews, reviews, family relationships, motherhood, death, spirituality, service delivery, unemployment... Each piece is imbued with that typical straight incisive truthfulness of the Zimbabweans, and the beauty of an artful country and culture that our country is known for. Enjoy!

USED, ABUSED and REFUSED, Part One

The plight of Zimbabwe's national liberation war veterans, 45 years on
Killian Mwanaka (aka Cde Ducas Fambai)

Writing about Zimbabwe's history, from British colonial rule, without mentioning the critical and decisive role played by the national liberation war veterans, would be erroneous. Although many strata of the population – mujibhas, chimbwidos, the general peasantry (povo), the intellectuals... – played an important role in fighting the Rhodesian forces, the task was auxiliary; it was the national liberation war veterans (as we call them today), who performed a pivotal role of confronting the Rhodesian forces with guns and other weapons of war. From their respective war zones across Zimbabwe as ZANLA (Zimbabwe African National Liberation Army) and ZIPRA (Zimbabwe People's Revolutionary Army), the fighters gallantly engaged the Rhodesian forces in the Second Chirumenga War that started, in earnest, in 1971 till the Lancaster House Conference of 1979, that succeeded in over-seeing a negotiated settlement for the independence of Zimbabwe.

The Zimbabwean national liberation war veterans (both ZANLA and ZIPRA), shall be imprinted in the annals of Zimbabwe's history as the bravest generation of young men and women who succeeded in defeating the colonial settlers pioneered by genocidal Cecil John Rhodes, the architect of colonialism in Southern Africa. As they gallantly fought the Rhodesian forces, thousands died and many were maimed. Sadly, this generation of brave fighters shall also go down in the history of Zimbabwe as the most maligned, despised and unrecognised among all Zimbabwe's generations, notwithstanding the sacrifice they made to liberate their country. This generation defeated the myth that the pink-man (the one you call white-man) is invincible. This generation, the history-makers of Zimbabwe, has been condemned to the dust-bin of the nation's history.

Euphoria and expectations

The first independence celebrations at Rufaro Stadium and elsewhere in the country, on 18 April 1980, were euphoric and consequently, expectations of what a free Zimbabwe would bring, were sky-high.

In this discourse, I shall narrow down my analysis of Zimbabwe's independence to the state of national liberation war veterans then and now. I shall write here as one of them as, indeed, I am one of the national liberation war veterans who fought the Rhodesian forces in the forests, mountains and valleys of Zimbabwe. I am writing from the perspective of one who is a national liberation war veteran from the ZANLA's side.

Firstly, let me lay bare my credentials. My home name is Killian Mwanaka and was named Ducas Fambai, as my nom-de-guerre, at Mgagao Training College, Iringa, Tanzania in December 1973 when I started military training at this most renowned ZANLA military training camp.

My analysis, of Zimbabwe's national liberation war veterans then and now, shall not be partisan or sectarian-leaning. I shall endeavour, as much as I can, to be objectively honest and factual, yet, I shall be fiercely and fearlessly brutal.

I decided to join ZANLA (instead of ZIPRA) in Francistown Botswana where I met the likes of Dominic Chinenge (Constant Chiwenga, current Zimbabwe Vice President), Perence Shiri (late former Zimbabwe's Minister of Agriculture) and Rtd. Brigadier General Flavion Danga (former Defence Attache in India 2018 – 2022). The trio had come from Mt. St. Mary's, Wedza, where they'd cut-short their education, in pursuit of the armed struggle to liberate Zimbabwe. I was coming from the United College of Education, Bulawayo teachers' training college, where I had gone to pursue a teaching course after secondary education at the prestigious Marist Brothers Secondary School, Nyanga.

With the trio (from Mt. St. Mary's, I mentioned above) and other cadres who included Comrades Tendai Pfepferere (Dr. Matthew Mudambo), Grey Mapondera (Everisto Mwatse), Felix Chemandiwe (Zacharia Moyo), we completed a gruelling six months' guerrilla warfare training under highly-skilled instructors of the likes of Comrades Dzinashe Machingura (Wilfred Mhanda), Kenneth Gwindingwi (John Gwitira), Gordon Mlambo, David Todhlana (Chrispen Mataire), Parker Chipowera (Bernard Chinyadza), Kenneth Taitezvi (Edson Nyarambi) and James Nyikadzinashe (Regis Muzadzi).

After training, I and others were deployed to the front and operated in the Nehanda Sector's Nyombwe Detachment (Mukumbura, Mt. Darwin, Madziwa and the surrounding areas). After my stint from the front in 1975, I was appointed Political Commissar for Chibawawa and, later, Doeroi refugee camps in Mozambique and promoted to ZANLA's member of the General Staff.

The conditions agreed at Lancaster House by the ZANU (Zimbabwe African National Union) and ZAPU (Zimbabwe African Peoples' Union) leadership signed on 21 December 1979, dictated that the national liberation war veterans be confined in assembly points during cease-fire with the Rhodesian forces.

The war veterans were a mix mainly of semi-literate peasants, secondary school-leavers and a sizable number of university-leavers. Considering that, in earnest, guerrilla warfare in Zimbabwe, spearheaded by ZANLA, started in the north-eastern part of the country (Centenary and Mount Darwin districts), in 1971, by comrades who included Rex Nhongo, Mayor Urimbo and Sarudzai Chinamaropa, young men and women cut-short their primary and secondary education, en-mass, to join the armed struggle. The north-eastern and eastern part of Zimbabwe, bordering Mozambique, was used by ZANLA militants to enter Zimbabwe. ZANLA leadership had earlier entered into an agreement with FRELIMO (Frente de Libertacao de Mozambique) to use Mozambique for bases and entrance into Zimbabwe. ZIPRA forces used the Zambian border to enter into Zimbabwe and operated in the north and north-western part of the country.

As the war intensified, spreading along the eastern part of the country, thousands of young men and women, mainly from schools such as St. Agustine's in Penhalonga, Hartzell in Old Mutare, Marist Brothers Nyanga, Mount Selinda, Chikore and many others, flocked into Mozambique.

Life in the camps

The recruits settled at Tembwe in Tete, Nyadzonia, Chimoio and Chibawawa as refugees. Chimoio would later be transformed into a military training camp. Recruits from these camps would be transported to Mgagao or Nachingweya in Tanzania, Libya and Ethiopia and other countries for military training. In these camps, the would-be fighters were taught political orientation which focussed on why they were fighting a guerrilla war against the Ian Smith minority regime and not less importantly, how the country would be administered when the enemy was defeated. The Political Commissars would relentlessly remind the comrades that Zimbabwe, like the Biblical Israel, was a country flowing with milk and honey. They (Political Commissars) would constantly quote socialist giants like Karl Marx, Frederick Engels, Lenin, Mao Tse Tung, Fidel Castro and Che Guevara. Socialism, a political-economic system, which supported the general masses, against the minority exploitative bourgeois capitalism, would be practised in a new Zimbabwe. With its abundant natural resorces, Zimbabwe would grow into a developed country with no poverty and exploitation of man by man. This inspired the cadres to the point that many demanded to be given guns and go to the front to fight the enemy even before undergoing military training.

An air of camaraderie prevailed in the camps as the new cadres called one another 'comrade'. They discarded their home names and were given Chimurenga names. The comrades in these camps, both in Mozambique and Zambia, endured all sorts of hardships. Food was scarce and there was not enough medication to treat malaria and other diseases. Girls' problems were compounded by a lack of adequate women's essential wear like bras, underwear and pads (I'm afraid all has to be told). The problem of 'matekenya' was unique especially in Mozambican camps. These were minute insects that penetrated into

13

one's tender part of the foot - in-between toes and the surrounding area - and laid eggs. As the small 'maggots' developed inside one's skin, it would make walking difficult, not speaking of them inflicting immense pain on the bearer. In the midst of their pain and suffering, the comrades kept marching forward with the determination and assurance that independent Zimbabwe would bring a befitting reward.

Inequality in the camps

A refugee camp such as Chibawawa and Doeroi had each, more than fifteen thousand comrades. These camps were administered by fighters who had seen action at the front called 'trainados' or 'veterans'. They were assisted by competent cadres selected from among the cadres. Among the comrades were teachers, medics, agricultural experts and other professionals who would form the core of a functional society at a camp.

Male and female comrades lived separately in 'barracks' made of pole and thatched with grass. Commanders, who constituted the administrative structure of the camp, lived in 'postos'. This was a privilege for the commanders because a commander would live alone in a 'posto' while the rest of the comrades were crammed in barracks.

They (commanders), had an added privilege of being provided with a 'guarda-posto' (assistant in Portuguese). The guarda-posto would assist with overseeing the needs of the commander assigned to him/her.

Commanders were privileged to dine at the 'mesa' (table in Portuguese) where they were served with enough and better food in contrast to the rest of the comrades who went by on a starvation diet due to a lack of adequate food in the camp. The commanders also enjoyed the privileges of having essential items - radios, clothes, toiletries (toothpaste, soap …) – which (items) were difficult to be available to the ordinary comrade. The above set-up was the same in all ZANLA camps in Mozambique, Zambia and Tanzania. Absolute equalitarianism was never near practised in our camps despite the political instructors fervently preaching it.

In retrospect, the inequality of life in our camps in Mozambique, Zambia and Tanzania, is the prototype of life that our government and party officials instituted in independent Zimbabwe, albeit on an outlandish monumental scale with complex dynamics. The creation of a super class structure that is ruling Zimbabwe today, that has produced billionaires, multi-millionaires and millionaires while most of the populace scrounge a living on less than a dollar per day, is partly our creation; we are decrying our own creation.

We raped our female comrades

The subject of rape, in our camps is one that, especially, male national liberation war veterans, would neither want to hear nor talked about. They vehemently deny it (rape) ever happened. Yet it indeed, did happen. Female comrades were raped. The reason male national liberation war veterans would rather the subject of raping women in our camps is not talked about is because they were the perpetrators. The culpability of raping their female counterparts makes them feel ashamed. On the other hand, female national liberation war veterans shy away from the subject because they feel talking about it is dehumanising and degrading on their person. Not talking about rape as it happened in our camps, because of the above reasons, would be stifling history; history must be told as it happened.

Clear cases of female war veterans being raped by their male comrades occurred at Nyadzonya, Refugee Camp. As refugees flocked at Nyadzonya in 1975, administration was initially in the hands of the FRELIMO authorities who controlled and managed the provision of food, blankets, clothing and other essentials. But they (FRELIMO officials) soon handed over the running of the camp to ZANLA commanders who appeared at the camp from the front. These commanders were led by Cdes Bombardiari, Saudi and Gutura. The four commanders ran Nyadzonya as their fiefdom. They harassed the comrades, imprisoning those they suspected of being 'vatengesi' (sell-outs). The suspects were made to confess that they were sent by the Rhodesians and ANC's Abel Muzorewa to spy on the revolution. Some comrades were forced to make false confessions to save their skin. Some were publicly flogged on the parade-ground and later incarcerated in 'chikarabotso' (prison). Meanwhile, Bombardiari and company lived a life of debauchery, drinking beer and smoking cigarettes and 'mbanje' bought from Chimoio and the surrounding Mozambican community. Bombardiari and his crew had become a law unto themselves as they would, in their drunken stupor, fire bullets into the air, prompting some comrades to flee camp. Bombardiari and crew's criminal shenanigans did not end here; they selected girls of their choice and brought them to their 'postos' and slept with them. Wowed and cowed by the AK rifles the commanders carried, no girl would say 'No!' lest they were labelled a sell-outs. Bombardiari and company are known to have raped dozens of girls each during their notorious reign at Nyadzonya. It was only after an authentic ZANU administration headed by Cde Munetsi was installed at Nyadzonya that the Bombardieri and Saudi's reign of terror came to an end. At learning of their misdeeds, Cde Munetsi had the four rogue commanders incarcerated at the camp's 'chikarabotso'. When Cde Rex Nhongo, member of ZANLA's High Command and senior to Cde Munetsi arrived at Nyadzonya, he had the three notorious commanders released.

Because there were no conventional judicial institutions in our camps, victims of rape, among female comrades, were powerless to bring their cases in the open.

Cases of rape did not only occur at the camps. As we wielded the AK and went about conducting war ventures in the operational areas, we exuded an aura of invincibility among the villagers who we rightly convinced the country would soon be independent. The girls (chimbwidos) who brought food and water and other essentials to the bases where we were 'hidden' would often fall victims of rape. No 'chimbwido' would say, 'No!' to the comrade who fancied her. Willy-nilly, she would sleep with the comrade for fear of the gun.

Many children were born due to the interaction of fighters and 'chimbwidos' in the operational zones. It is sad that some of these children would never know their fathers due to the mishaps of the war.

To those (especially male national liberation war veterans) who say rape in our camps did not happen, it is time we face and accept the truth and above all, apologise. On behalf of Cdes Bombardiari, Saudi and Gutura and all those who, in plain sight, perpetrated this despicable and inhuman act on our hapless female comrades, all male national liberation war veterans must hang their heads in shame and unreservedly apologise to our female national liberation war veterans, most of who have lived with the trauma and stigma of being raped for over forty years

Dear Emerson Mnangagwa:
Free and Fair Elections!
Tendai Rinos Mwanaka

"What is your name, Skull?"

T here are a couple of years at school I want to talk to you about. There is this year we got a really difficult insufferable Head boy at school. He was too strict. Even if you were friends with him, if he found you on the wrong end of the school rules, he will book you for punishment. And I had my full share of these bookings and detentions. Yes, I admit I was a difficult student. But what I also realized, even for those who were never punished by this head boy, they still didn't like him. Deep down all this insufferable strictness, he was driven by a streak of cruelty. He wallowed in cruelty. The students finally realized this about him. Even on issues where the whole student body was fighting against the administrators, he always found his side with the administrators, yet his other job was to represent the students to the powers that be. So the students ended up resenting him. The students liked his deputy who was a far better person, wished the deputy was the one on the top. This deputy treated us as adults, respectfully. But the deputy never got the chance to lead us. With the end of this head boy's term of office we selected another head boy. What the old head boy had made us feel was that office was against the students; we distrusted it, so that this new head boy took off with a student body that already despised the office he was taking over. We didn't give him time to adjust, and show us what he was all about. We distrusted him straight off. We shut him out, we resented him. And he responded exactly like the previous head boy. He punished us. He blocked us. He harassed us and we wished his deputy would get a chance to lead us. But the deputy can only become the head

19

boy only if the head boy leaves his office during his term of office. At school that was highly unlikely, so we had to figure out a way to deal with that, and moved on with our lives.

Emerson, you are the second head boy at this school we are enrolled in for all our lives. This school has a name; Zimbabwe. Emerson you have inherited an office that we despised, that we don't like because that office was made a monster by Robert Mugabe. It is so offensive to us. Robert used that office to punish us, to kill us, to maim us, to destroy our economy and country, to make us feel like we were nobodies in our school. It's only him we had to listen to and obey. We learned to hate Robert and the office of the president. Don't be fooled into thinking we only hated Robert. We hated the whole system, the whole government. We never wished for you to take over like we wished those deputy head boys to take over at school so many moons ago. You were Robert. You are Robert. Here is a tale I want to share with you, Emerson

*****

Some time ago, not so long ago there was this man who felt he had shadows he didn't understand. He told himself there were shadows that spoke to him when he was asleep but never really grasped what they wanted him to do. And then they started to speak to him even when he was awake, when he was listening, when he wasn't listening. He heard those shadows speaking deep inside himself. The voices of which were an amalgam of light and shadows flickering, sizzling him with restlessness he didn't understand or know how to deal with. They told him he had to go to a Well by the end of the village, a disused, dumped Well, where naught kids circled around it by the close of the day, singing, calling the old prophet to come and awash them with gold.

There is a story, a story in a story, a legend that the Well had dried in another lifetime with the death of an old prophet man of this village when he fell in this Well. It was said the prophet man had tried to retrieve a blood tree (Mubvamaropa tree) box

that was full of gold. So that, even when the villagers managed to retrieve the dead body of this prophet, it was thought the Well was cursed, yet some thought a ceremony dance around this Well helped to soften the restlessness and hunger inside souls, a hunger for wealth, isn't that the only hunger that really drive us? These kids were propagating this folklore, though playfully, but in this old man the voice kept whispering to him to go to the Well. It told him that deep inside the Well there was definitely a Mubvamaropa tree box full of treasures. The voice told him to go to the Well and excavate this treasure trove.

This man, deep in his dreams left for the Well. He knew he had to listen to this voice and free himself from its restlessness. He had to go there to find wealth for himself and his people. In this night the moon was a bruise on the skies, it emitted reddish wounds of flowers of light, the whole night was in bubbles of voices beckoning, wishing him to keep going, to keep moving, and he could only obey these voices. He couldn't make himself to stop. He got to this Well in the early hours of morning. It was surreal, he searched around for the rope the people of that far off time had used to excavate the old prophet man with and he found it was still there, waiting for him like one left over log to use to light up a fire in a world with no trees. He took a small stone and threw it into the Well to measure how deep the Well was; by noting the time it took for the stone to hit the box of treasure. The thumb hit of this mubvamaropa tree told him the rope was long enough to reach the bottoms. He immersed the rope with a hook attacked to its end into the Well. He felt it hit something and he felt it hook it. He started drawing it out. He felt the weight. He knew he had finally rounded up on his voices. The expectations he had for the treasures! He kept drawing it until something hang on top of the Well's mouth. It had the shape... Not of a box! He reached his hand to touch it, to see it. He was asleep so he couldn't really see it with his shut eyes, but he used his fingers to feel it, to see it. His hands closed on this object. He touches two holes on its top; and a opening below them belies a mouth. He knew it was the skull he was holding. He asks this skull,

WHAT'S YOUR NAME, SKULL? But the skull didn't answer him. He was angry and like Moses throwing the tablets on the ground in the bible, he threw it on the ground. He cried to the space above him
WHERE IS MY BOX OF WEALTH, WHY DID YOU SEND ME THIS SKULL?
Nothing answers him. He takes the skull in his hands, he looks at it again with his fingers, and he felt a song in his heart telling him it was the skull of his mentor. The skull looked familiar, like his head on his body. He touches his head, he felt he was touching his mentor's head. So he looked at the skull again and tears begun flowing down his face. The front porch of his brain knew he was himself in this skull. He was the skull. He asks the skull again, softly.
What is your name, Skull?
He only heard his own voice askance.
He took the skull and put it on his head, and it fitted him well. He knew he was the skull.

This is how we know you are the skull. It is your story's life, Emerson. Don't ask us how we came to know of this, we only know! This is how we know you are Robert. This is how we know we are dealing with Robert's skull. No, Emerson we are not going to give you time. No, I have no reason to think you will be different from your skull. Don't forget we know you were with Robert at the Well, trying to excavate the box full of wealth in Marange, and that you helped him make us hate the office of the president, the government. Don't be surprised when everything you do or touch is going to create noise, anger, bitterness and displeasure with the people. What are the sounds for but to hear what isn't there. It's your voice you will be hearing.

Dear president, our apologies, we will chop you off the living skull on your head.

You are Robert Mugabe. It's you who hurt us for 37 years. It's you who destroyed the country for 37 years. The country is empty. I think if I were to go home now and knock on the Zimbabwean blue skies, I would hear the hallow sound of my own empty hands penning this missive in all that Zimbabwean blue. It's you who stole the elections for 37 years; it's you who burned down our homes, maimed people who were against you. If you think I am fibbing go to Kwekwe today and ask the people there what they think of you. Ask the Kwekwe people who burned down Blessing Chebundo's home, who killed a number of activists in Kwekwe. Emerson, it's you who killed thousands of the Matabele people. Despite the fact that you are always saying it's not you who led the genocide, ask the Matabele people who killed their families. They know it's you. The whole country knows it's you. Yes, we know they were a lot of people involved in that madness (Sidney Sekeremayi, Perence Shiri, Solomon Mujuru and the army, Edson Shirihuru, Kevin Woods, Menard Muzariri, the CIO people, and you Emerson, Robert Mugabe, his deputy "Nehanda Nyakasikana" Muzenda and cabinet, even Chiwengwa… all these are a closeted plausibility of chihauhaus, come back Joshua Nkomo!). Oh, Chiwenga can as well say what you saying too, to excuse himself since he was at the 1 Infantry Brigade in Bulawayo not the monster 5 Infantry brigade based in Kwekwe that Perence Shiri lead as they grounded down the Matebele people. Chiwengwa provided support to Shiri's 5 Brigade. You two can say you were not there when you were there, but we all know it's a lie. Even a wind takes with it evidence of where it has been. Violence is a product of systemlessness as much as a pillar of lootercracy, Emerson. Who did the target killing of the politicians and leaders of the Gukurahundi? It's the CIO. Who tried to kill Nkomo as he skirted out of the country in woman dressing, running from your thugs the CIO who were on his tail. You were the minister of security, Emerson. Tell us why Mugabe fired you, if you were not involved. Don't think we are such fools

23

we will accept you didn't know what your subordinates like Kevin Woods were doing in the ministry you led. Don't think we are dump goats we don't know the army couldn't have done that work without the intelligence knowledge it got from the CIO. It is the CIO that helped the army extirpate the Matabele. You were the head of the organisation, you crushed them in your hands, you are covered in blood that dripped from the people to become empty shells, like testimony. So don't tell us lies, no amount of lies will ever make us think of you differently as your skull, Robert. A caterpillar out of botulism does not become a butterfly. So stop trying to persuade us you are clean, prove it. Come out clean. Tell us what really happened in Matabeleland. This experiment is to see who has been killing us, Emerson. The experiment is about a lot I don't know, the experiment is about silent things talking in the dark of now. You are Robert and the Zimbabweans have no engagement rings for you man; they can't commit themselves to a thug boss!

Emerson, it's you who killed your rivalries and Robert's rivalries in the ZANUPF power soaps we have come to expect over the years. It is you who has pushed out those who blocked your ambitions to one day succeed Robert and come to terms with your voices inside you. It's you who we blame for the killing of Solomon Mujuru, Learnmore Jongwe, the generals, the political commissars (Movern Mahachi, Elliot Manyika, Border Gezi), and everyone who was against your ambitions and your skull, Robert. It's you we blame for everything that Zimbabwe is; oh we might as well blame you for global warming! Let my pen reveal what you can't reveal to us and if I am free to speak loosely, the predator could easily be revealed. It's you who forced Robert to take farms from the whites, you who gutted the white people. Don't think you can fool us now when you say you have changed, that you now want the white people back. A crow bird, no matter how much it cleans itself, is always black.

Do you know each pattern is different, like a snowflake but none is as cold as you are? It's you who pushed Robert to send our soldiers to the DRC to fight a war that has never benefited the generality of Zimbabweans, but rather depleted every foreign currency reserve the country had and pushed us into inflation. It's you who looted the DRC of its diamonds and made billions out of that Lootercracy. Ask the United Nations, they know your money was from blood diamonds you looted in the DRC and at that Well in Marange. It's you Emerson who stole elections that the opposition had won in 2008. Wasn't that you we heard who told your skull that he wasn't going anywhere, and took the whole country to ransom as you played with the work of our pens until Chiwenga's gun ruled us again? Emerson, it's you who helped create the securocratic leadership style that now subject us to poverty, it's you who re-created the monster Joint Operations Command that has run the country, de facto basis since year 2000.

It's you Emerson who took the country through a coup just a few weeks ago, and hauled your skull to the ground. You opened your big mouth which can only be described as that of a comic book character, gulped everything down at once. Didn't we hear you from foreign lands asking the skull what his name was? Didn't we hear your voice in the voice of your chummy Chiwenga asking Robert who his name was whilst his distance from our streets disagreed with us, by imprisoning Robert in his beautiful blue roof casket? With frightening speed, actions took hold of Robert in a matter of a few days. Didn't you repeatedly lie to us that it wasn't a coup, didn't you say it had no name. You called it operation restore order, you called it a coup which was not a coup, you called it capturing thieves surrounding the president, so why did you capture the skull into your hands and took it to be yours, why did you fit the skull on your head at the end of the coup. Yes, there was so much love lost between Robert and us. We had buried our love of Robert so many years ago like that village had buried the body of their prophet who had died in that Well.

But we supported you, we danced around the Well with you Emerson, and we were little children looking for something we didn't know, whittling away at the silhouette that had kept us captive so that the night of his resignation we all might sail into drinks and talk and the shared adulations of this small army of joy, the vibrations, the vibe, *buzz, bizz bizz*, the fear, and in the morning the sweepers would follow the parade march. But you hijacked that dream for us too. Even though we danced with you we knew the Well was not clean. We knew you were not clean. We supported you because we felt it was better to deal out one monster at a time. Now Robert is gone, don't think we are fools to think his Mugabeism is buried with his body, no. You have his skull on your head, Emerson. We still see the shadows. We know ZANUPF is a group of look alikes/ dress alikes/ think alikes/ looter alikes, near insanity Bono rock music look alikes who concocted to distance themselves from their boss when the people called it quits, and your ZANUPF supporters even know you are interchangeable, and that when these look alikes are kicked, other Robert Mugabe look alikes will take over like allusions of the Mussolinis eating Ethiopian checken (chicken) bones in the form of the Mengestus. You are just a new leader of an old sect. We even know you are more dangerous than Robert; that Mugabe's imaginations have hybridized into monster crops in you! Yet it's better to deal with the head of the snake than its tails that we have been dealing with all along. Now, you are out on the open.

We are going to fight you until you are gone too. We are on you, until we eat your footsteps in our sleep. I cast out a proud call to you Emerson;

we will swallow stones, grasses, poison, bitterness, molasses, stuff our mouths with emptiness, depth and height for the next few months until the elections. Emerson, we will consume birds, beasts, locusts, monsters, fish, glue, sadza, wind clay salt, ripples…, until we become this for you, stone and only stone, until we push you out too. We know it is good to be alive, even on a leash, to test our reflexes. You are from ZANUPF. So as far as we concerned we gave you 37 years and you rundown the country. 37! 37! 37! We are not going to give you another 37 years to ruin us further. We have waited too long for uhuru, and the georgics of waiting beyond now are time as a torn cloth. We know you have nothing to offer us. We know you can only resort to buying our votes in the next 8 months or so until the elections. We see you have started the "buying us" programme. You think it impresses us that you have refused to use Robert's chariot of fire, the limousine, gold plated with the black gold of the blood he bleed from us over the years as he paraded and cocked all over our roads. Of course, your emergence demand a makeover that would seem to impart change, simplicity and maturity, perhaps a whiff of Africa's present darling, a magufulication! If you think it impresses us you cut back your congress expenditure from 8 mil to 2 mil. If you think we have bought into those promises you made that you are now born again and should be absolved for killings you did under Robert, and that you now want the white people back, now that you have the crown, making it seem as if it was Mugabe only who was wrong all along. If you wanted this done you should have done it yesterday. Everyone knows Mugabe was against farm invasions, tried to fight you and the goons to leave the farms. If you think we can easily buy into this fluffy thing that you now want to compensate the whites for taking their farms forcefully, with what money, Emerson. I will come to that later (letter). If you want it done right now put pride aside man, and tell us the truth and pray to space. Achieve a better form of purity, Emerson! If you think we have bought into your lies that you now want to resuscitate the economy you destroyed, that you have started by cutting down the number of ministries in your government, and if I may ask you, why is there some process toward militarizing the government. This unassembled cabinet that is waiting for its own loot in this mineral rich country! I might come back to that, no promises. Emerson, just know that all that you have done or purporting you will do doesn't impress us. First thing first, Emerson!

We have an election next year. Make that right, first of all. Give us a free and fair election. Win or lose it fairly, then if you win fairly we will start trusting your good intentions. Rest awhile; we are not even there yet, not even with a fair election. There are sins you have to apologize and pay for, for humankind's swelling expenses. I will come to that later. Let's stay on the elections now. I said we know all these promises were to buy us into believing you now care for us as we toward the elections. Whereas your skull gave us food and agric implements, sometimes used panties to cloth up our open business, you thought you could better your skull by offering us what we have clamored for all along to fill up our flesh, thus to flesh up your skull too. I said we know you are not the deputy head boy of this school. You are Robert, the head boy!

On free and fair elections here are the areas I want you to right. Fire Rita Makarau and her gang at ZEC. We know she is the dust that clung around the skull you have in your hands. She is Robert's lapdog, she stole the 2013 election for Robert, awarding him and his party ZANUPF the two thirds majority they now have. Just think of it? How could your old decaying skull get a two thirds majority in a village that so hated the shadows of your skulls. No, she has to go. The second issue is ZEC should be totally independent, chosen by civil society institutions like the Judiciary Service Commission, or be chosen by the Parly, with equal representation of parties that constitute our Parly. Not by the executive, not by the immediate players, not by oncoming players. The Registrar General is another public office that needs to be removed from your tentacles. Let's have the Parly overseeing that one too, or the judiciary.

The next reform area is on the military and security establishment. Zimbabwe is now a blank terrain, surrounded by two armies, one wields a gun and another, a pen. We want the army off our political processes. Tell Chiwenga and his power grabbing goons to go back to the barracks. Tell those monsters to focus their energies on military issues, not political processes. We need a law that makes it clear that its treason for the army to enter our streets to temper with political process, payable by jail sentence. If they have nothing to do at the barracks, they should help in the construction of schools, clinics, roads etc. If they are tired of mooching off our taxes, if they are tired of training without a fight to engage in, export them to the world over, the world is full of strife. It would earn us foreign currency. Employ them to farm the millions of hectors that remain uncultivated every year and grow our agricultural industry and other industries. Apparently those goats are employable and there is a lot that needs to be done to build back Zimbabwe. They should leave politics to politicians, law to lawmakers and judiciary, theirs is military. We don't have a war in Zimbabwe. Nobody is killing the other in Zimbabwe. Zimbabwe has next to nothing possibility of degenerating into a war situation like Somalia which your chummy used as the cry call to enter the streets. We are civilized. We don't kill each other in Zimbabwe. This is not bloody Central or West Africa! Emerson, the military needs to be reformed, and those who have nothing to do should be retired. The heads of the military have to be retired too. We need new thinking, fresh perspectives in this organisation. We have over 30 000 active soldiers- that's too much for a country as small a Zimbabwe, a country that has no possibility of generating a war. What do we need all those soldiers for? There is nobody in the SADC region who wants to attack us, we don't even have any territorial dispute with any country in the SADC. And on top of that we have over 22 000 reserve soldiers in the form of war veterans, and these have been used to destabilize us, destroy opposition parties and make Zimbabwe ungovernable by messing with our political processes. Retire all these veterans, too. They have no use. Those who want to be politicians, let them do that on a personal level, not using our taxes to rape us further. We need a small highly technological and advanced force that focuses on their mandates in the constitution. It's no longer a game of numbers nowadays. Look at American wars of the last few years. They are winning fights without deploying a lot of soldiers on the ground. Cull this lot. We need about 15 000 soldiers for the size of Zimbabwe. Still on security reforms, the police and civil security establishment needs reforms. Their mandates are to protect the civilians and uphold the law. They should move from the police state that they are now and have made Zimbabwe to be, into a people state police. The CIO should focus on country security not politicians security, or party games that they are involved in.

The next reform area I want see done before the elections is on the media. Open up the airwaves. Licence more players in this important field. Make this "fourth organ" of state strong and independent. We need new independent broadcasters. For us to still have 1 TV station, 37 years down the line is an insult to us. For us to still have only 6 national radio stations that are all controlled by the government, one way or another is an insult. For us to have very few local community radio stations is simply bad. Open up the airwaves and leave the journalists and media people to do their jobs in a free and fair environment, not to report according to party lines. ZANUPF is not Zimbabwe. I know that because I didn't see the memo that changed Zimbabwe to be ZANUPF republic. The media's job is to serve the people not politicians. Allow free and fair reporting on the national broadcaster, give competing parties into the next year's elections a fair share of airwaves time. Leave the internet alone. Leave people to express what they think in these internet social platforms. Let the information be shared in a free and fair way. It's laughable you have a ministry that focuses on that. I wonder what flimsy ministry you are going to create next, the ministry for love!

The other reform area is on the commission that deals with constituency demarcation. The job should be given to an independent organisation, independent from your executive power mongering hands. The constituency delimitation and demarcation should be overseen by Parly or judiciary appointed organization. We know how you have used this exercise to give yourself and your party unfair advantage over opposition parties. This is how you got two thirds majority in the Parly now. How did I come to this when I am not a statistician? When I realized the impossibility of counting to infinity the millions in Zimbabwe, I have decided to vomit these numbers. It's a big flat joke to think that a city like Chitungwiza that crawls with people from every hole, over 1.5 million people, will have 5 constituencies, yet a district like Gokwe will have the equal number of constituencies. And this capital should be damned-Harare, which has plus 2 million people has not more than 20 constituencies yet provinces with fewer people than Harare have more constituencies. Don't lie to us that three major urban centers (Harare, Chitungwiza and Bulawayo) with more than 4 million people combined together would not even have a fifth of the constituencies of Zimbabwe. 4 million people is almost a third of Zimbabwe's population. Protest all you want, but there is a grain of truth in these vomits. Let the statistician illuminate this beyond mathematical doubt, if you want. We know you and your party have used this organisation to give more constituencies to rural areas that have more ZANUPF supporters than those that are predominantly opposition. Get your power mongering hands off this cake, Emerson.

The next port of call is the judiciary. I find a judiciary that legitimatizes a coup suspect. A coup is a coup, that's the only name it is known by; otherwise we might as well call it a soup. We all stumbled as we were struck in the shock of it! But a simple truth is soldiers in a constitutional democracy can only come into the streets in times of war or civil emergences, not to right a party. Chiwenga was clear why he decided to enter our streets from the beginning of it. He wanted to clean up the mess in the ZANUPF party, period. What happened later with major general SB Moyo is known as sanitizing a wrong. I have said it before ZANUPF is not a country. Why didn't he enter the streets to right the MDC when it had power problems? We have an election to sort the country, not the army. And the sick thing is if a judiciary is blind to how the law works, how are we going to have faith in such an institution like that. Chiwenga is not the commander-in-chief of Zimbabwe Defense Forces. Mugabe was the boss. So for Chiwenga to come into our streets it had to be signed off by the president. It was Mugabe who had the right to allow the soldiers to invade the streets and break down government as they did. It doesn't matter if it was for the right causes or wrong causes. It's a wrong precedent the army and courts have set. What if the same army decides, in the future, to invade the streets again without your consent and hold the country by the gun? It's dangerous to have an army that doesn't operate under the country's constitution. There is nothing legal about that coup. So we need an overhaul of our judiciary. We want them to be independent of the executive levers and authority, to be able to safeguard our constitution against the monster that invaded our streets. The military that is bend on instituting what they want on the electorate and a conniving ruling party and cowering judiciary. Make no mistake, Emerson; a day will reckon when someone in your party will use the same army to hold you at gunpoint like they did to Robert and call it a coup that is not a coup, and with a stupid judiciary like the one that has just sanitized the coup this army will remove you from power too.

The other reform area is to do with the electoral law. Let's have an independent justice body that deals with the election contestation issues. Don't forget every time there was a dispute this judiciary has just sat on the cases that the opposition had brought to the courts. None have been dealt with; some never saw a court date. It took the judiciary 5 years to the next election to not decide the 2002, and 2005 election disputes, and then the cases became null and void as another election became due. We need an election body made up of representatives of several facets of the government, country, parties, experts, civil society, NGOs, local authorities, religious groupings…, and these would decide on elections matters and do so before a president-elect is inaugurated. There is no free and fair election in subjecting the electorate to a president who has won a disputed election.

The last issue I want to touch on is of allowing observers and monitors to observe and monitor our elections. Allow all those who want to come to observe to come. Allow and protect party monitors to monitor elections without fear for their lives. We want to see an election where the opposition can be able to deploy monitors in areas like Muzarabani and Uzumba Maramba Pfungwe without fear for their lives. Without which, don't lie to us and your cohorts of ZANUPF supporters like SADC and AU that the election has been free and fair

These are areas I want to see tackled before elections next year. As you can see, Emerson, it's a lot of work that needs your focus, rather than trite issues like you have refused to use the limousine crap. We know ZANUPF party is a master at deflecting people's views to buy into an illusion that things are now fine to win over their vote. Those are only trapdoors that don't get us home. Mugabe's regime was our knowledge pond: we are graduates revolting.

Code to the core, Mnangagwa you do so move, always you do so move man, to maim us, and now you do so move, you move to soothe us. We know this gimmick; we know this thing about limousine, of catching the said to be thieves around the presidency is just useless noise. You are hiding from the election reform issues, cradling to your old ways, hiding, stealing, thuggery... If you are really serious about growing Zimbabwe again, do the reforms first and give us a free and fair election for the first time. If you win as I have noted that before we will support you to the hilt as you rebuilt the country you destroyed. It's a museum of things for us to forget too, always afraid we might forget the distance we have travelled, the trouble of stopping now. Oh we can't afford to stop now. There are no stops in these roads of gravel. The angry gestures over our former authorities and current authorities in the letter are only means in the roads we are travelling in. These roads of gravel we are travelling in will lead to freedom of the constructions of our dreams. We are in phases of tilling and harvesting, November's rain fire lures us to our freedoms.

We will accept you on one condition! First of all declare what you have, and how you got it. Tell us how much you looted from that Well in Marange. Everyone in your new government should do that too. If you can at least prove to us what happened to the 15 billion you found in that Mubvamaropa box in the Well in Marange, then we will believe all this noise. I said first of all pay back what you stole, show us what you benefited from through corruption, push your cabal in the ZANUPF to declare what they benefited from through corruption, and then the whole country will do likewise. Otherwise this is just a sad excuse you are using to blindfold us to steal an election with, and when you have won then you will revert back to business as usual in something that is continuous, alooter continue. Oh don't confuse democracy and alootercracy, even if they both end in –acy…no, not that! I stop it, I am subjected!

Another gimmick you have narrowed on is the land issue. You know it is an emotional issue. You have promised the white people you are going to pay them for stealing their lands. Who is going to pay for that? I never got a piece of land from that exercise, never stole land from the white people, never benefited from it, in fact the bulk of the country didn't benefit from that, why must our taxes be used to pay for what we never benefited from. Rather the exercise has made the whole country poor. Those who looted the farms must pay the white people for the loot. We are waiting for the land reform audit. Those who have more than 1 farm, must return these to the white people they displaced to loot. They are practically hundreds, if not thousands of these farms that can be returned to their rightful owners before you start making us pay for your looting. How can we Zimbabweans be made to compensate white people to allow people like Robert Mugabe, Edna Madzongwe, Shuvai Mahofa to keep more than 5 farms each, farms they are not even using. Don't forget when you arm-twisted your skull to enter the farms and allow your goons to displace the white people you lied to us that you will each only get a farm, not 5, not 14 for one person. If you want to earn our respect, stop subjecting us under taxes we didn't benefit from. It's us people who have suffered from these stupid policies like the land invasion. You meted poverty on us. And we have become who we are and learned how to cry

35

and produce material evidence of our sadness. Don't think we will be patient as you continue subjecting us to this callousness. We are wild now, we are not afraid of your tanks. Look, we are saying, "we are sad", we are hurt enough, and we won't accept more pain. You and your band of crooks benefited from the land reform, so please payback the whites from the rent you have accrued from using those farms for nearly 20 years. There is no excuse why you can't payback the white people what you stole from them. We see this for what it is. It's another election gimmick.

In the meanwhile open up industry, clean up the mess you created with the indigenization programme. Chunk that law into the Robert Mugabe dustbin. Create attractive investment opportunities and environments in the country to allow industry to grow. Create free tax zones in the country. Use the Silicon Valley/ Shanghai method that has made China and the USA super rich, allow investors to invest in tax free heavens, especially companies that employ more people, thus this will cut back on unemployment rates and boast government tax base. Focus on creating solid banking structures in Zimbabwe, stabilize the currency, and control the financial sector. Clean up the mess at the mining sector; make it secure for investments and also secure our taxes from the mining sector. We can't afford to lose another 15 billion dollars. Make tourism and services industries grow. This is an easy cash cow as they are fewer investments involved to make money in this sector, than in industry, mining and agriculture. Clean up our image in the international community. This will encourage more tourists to visit. We have enough tourist attractions sites to make Zimbabwe a world class tourist destination centre.

As you can see there is a lot we want you to do before we warm up to you, and you don't have time or our patience. Of course we will tolerate you for next few months problematically; don't forget a hungry educated pen is both a gun and pen. First of all, and I repeat it, give us free and fair elections!

I think I am a no one or nation and this outrage is justified, there is no purpose of nation if it doesn't allow a frame where happiness zigzags with beauty.

This letter has two distinct cries. One is called *Chiduce*, an omen of good, and the other is *Huitreu*, which is extremely unfavourable! Ask Frank Herbert. Hope you have heard both cries.

Thank you, Ndinotenda, Ngiyabonga, to the skull!

The philosophies of negativity of home as captured by poetry in the 21st Century

Tinashe Muchuri

What is home? Where is home? Is home a geographical space on earth or a perspective taking into consideration of pan-Africanism where Africans take the whole continent as a home for everyone? Where is home considering the call for one people one world through globalisation? Different scholars give home differing definitions. Brian Chikwava in his debut novel 'Harare North' refer to home as just a state of mind. The compilers of The Power of Ideas section in McDougal Littel Literature describes home as not the house one lives in but a place wherever one feels most comfortable and secure.

Reading through Batsirai Chigama's title poem to her debut poetry collection, *gather the children* in which she ask Africa and individual countries in the continent to gather children back home from the raging fires of South Africa, my anxiety of what home is was intrigued and was soon send on a long tour of poetry by Chigama's peers during the period her *gather the children* is interrogating.

Instead of finding an answer the poets send me through conversations and dialogues they had in different anthologies and collections which revolve around the question what is home and where is home? Is the home in 21st century still the same as that of the 19th century and beyond?

Most of the voices in poems published in the era that inspires Chigama and her peers were worried of a home that was disintegrating and falling apart, where children were no longer interested and proud to live and cherish home yet others felt it is

38

good for home to be left and sometimes visit those still feel the place habitable.

According to the voice in Edmond Shonhiwa's poem, *The Inferno echoes* which speaks to the xenophobic attacks of migrant workers by South Africans in the year 2008, Africa is home to every son and daughter of the continent but surprisingly other brothers and sisters were at the throat of their kith and kin. The voice asks why?

"This Africa is our mamaland
But you cast my children into the inferno
Where they diminish into ashes
Why, brother Azania, Why?"

Azania is the name that the liberation parties were proposing to rename South Africa after attaining majority rule from apartheid which never was to be. The voice asks has the brother forgotten that this home is for everyone.

A voice in Audrey Lindani Mutinhiri's poem *'Can we have One Africa?'* concur that indeed Africa is home for every African as it reminds the world and everyone with the ears to hear that;

"We are one
We are all Africa's children
We cannot suffer injustice,
From both oppressors and our brothers!"

Instead of the brothers in South Africa to love their brother they played the role of Cain of the Holly Bible who killed his brother, accusing him of receiving honour before God. The South Africans seem to have forgotten that theirs is not a home for them alone but a home for all Africans. Therefore setting their kith and kin on fire was not a good act. With the historical accounts of Bantu migration where people are said to have moved from the area of the Great

Lakes stretching down to the South where they moved again northwards running away from Tshaka Zulu during the Nguni incursion, this assertion seem to confirm the history.

But this torture and denial by brothers and people around the world doesn't stop the voice in Noreen Sadziwa's poem, *"My Dream Home"* which speaks to the plight of woman regarded barren and childless in a country where people believe a young sister's children are the elder sister's children. Where has our Ubuntu/unhu/vumunhu/vunhu gone to? Home is here symbolised as the barren mother whose children run away from. Children of Africa are scattered all over the world because mother is not gathering enough food to sustain her children's lives. The same children even as they grow into adults fails to stand by mother as they run to other homes where children of those mothers are helping shape the beauty of their mothers and women. And Africa is surviving on imports and heavily indebted because of borrowing and borrowing.

The voice hears the woman crying;

"A woman wails
It's the order of the day
Abused because she is barren."

The barren woman knows no peace, bile is poured on her wounds, being reopened everyday by venom filled words thrown at her by the people foreign and local. But this is not the home that the voice in the poem dreams of? This home of wailing women is not home. How can it be home when there is wailing voices that indicates to misunderstanding, toiling, warring, discomfort, and despair reigned by fear?

The voice in Mutinhiri's poem '*Family I Have None*' is mourning the absence of home because she is also barren and accused of causing her own plight. If home is home because of the presence of women in it, women alone without men also wail as there are other things, chores, jobs that are done by men only for the home to be inhabitable. This is a voice of homelessness person living as a squatter in a home that is said to be for everyone yet this voice lives in squalid conditions.

"I have wandered and slept in the streets
Under cardboard boxes and plastics
I have been the recipient on the litter
I have been called names,
'Mzawangendaba'.

Where one comes from, or the land of migrant workers' birth is always under fire for neglecting their children, surrendering the best labour and brains to menial jobs in foreign lands where some come back with no glittering riches that attracted them to, in some instances, illegally cross the border, is what the voice in Lilian Dube's poem 'He is Back': which illustrate that the greener pastures attracting children to foreign lands is not all that green as seen from afar.

"He left home
And two unborn sons
Five years ago
Skipped the border
Landed in Yeoville
Or was it Hillbrow?"

The narrator of the story is not even aware of the facts because the man who has just returned has not been in contact with home. Many people have gone and disappeared and they never communicated with people back in the villages and sometimes were assumed dead, or consumed by the vast waters of Limpopo River. The voice continues to describe the state that the person has come back home in. Home to some people is the place to which they get buried. This is the place they will lay forever, which others call the rest place while another group of people call it a place of birth and others say it is a place where one is sheltered.

And the voice in Dube's poem ends with;

"He came back
Three days ago-
There is he
There, face up
In the roughhewn
Coffin that has just
Bankrupted his mother –"

Here we can see a dialogue of voices thinking and asking the same questions, interrogating the era and painting agonies of the time with colours of pain. The voice in Mgcini Nyoni's poem, *'Ten years across the Limpopo'* is a dialogue as they seem sitting at a bridge sharing intoxicating Bronko, the Bronclear cough Syrup in Dube's poem, as it affirms the same plight of people who went to the diaspora and come back to their place of birth with nothing on them except sickness and a hope for a decent burial, costing those who were left behind. These are the people who regard home as a burial place they come to only when death beckons.

"What he brought back home is this:
A fruit knife
Known as okapi
The clothes on his back
A small radio
And the deadly
disease that's doggedly

eating him."

The voice in Charles Mungoshi's *'The Man Who Ran Away From Pain'* paints a picture of those people who ran away from home, whose eyes have been opened and now they have realised how pain is universal. Always get the unexpected results. Some find the going tougher than from the situation they ran away from.

"He ran away from home
Where, he thought, all pain
Began.
He went to another country
Where he discovered
The pain of leaving home."

Can this be said of those hiding away from the authorities of the countries of their economic refuge fearing being deported back with nothing on them or those holding onto asylum, gotten through the lying tooth? The voice here points to home as the place of birth.

Maybe this is the reason why the voice in Tinashe Mushakavanhu's poem 'Tomorrow is long coming' is lamenting of the pain of leaving home, where it says;

"Homesickness is a bird that sings to dawn
While it's dark. Is the tree outside a forest
To itself? Or time frozen in obeisance?"

And another voice in Mushakavanhu's poem 'In the House of Exile' stays in fear as the town that the voice ran to is not embracing. Only the forest or the trees are embracing as they don't chose to whom among the citizens and residents will inhale their oxygen. Could this be the genesis of xenophobic attack? Why is the world not home for every human being?

"This town I have adopted
Snoops at me suspiciously
Veiled in the colour of its skin
Blind to my dark present
Only the green breathes
Clean air."

Here is where the voice in Chigama's 'gather the children' instructs mother to gather her children. The voice is not concerned about those said to be prodigal sons and daughters but the ones mother let go after failing to feed them.

"I mean the ones you exiled, choked with despair
Drove across borders with sjamboks of hunger
Now they gingerly carry the stipes
Even as death surrounds them."

One would ask though whether mother is that selective of her children. Does mother select to dine with the good or embrace all her children hoping they will change for the better? If the home becomes selective, is it home then?

As for the voice in Ignatius Mabasa's poem 'Anxious Land' the 'land has fallen and there is no place to call home', as it accuses some fool who have decided to hang Zimbabwe which most people were calling home. The voice further alleges that the fool hung Zimbabwe's dirty without washing her linen or even bathing her body. Besides the home that is physical, the voice also talks about a spiritual home promised to congregants by the Word of God through the coming of Jesus Christ.

"If we don't slump, like fallen baobab,
We will never fall again

Until Christ's Kingdom comes.
For when He comes
There shall not be left one stone upon another,
That shall not be thrown down."

This voice speaks of a spiritual home promised with the coming of Jesus Christ.

Or is home the nest called by a voice in David Mungoshi's poem 'The Empty Nest' in which new lessons has been learnt, that human beings are like birds and that they own nests which they sometimes should fly away from to rest from the routine. Is it routine of foodlessness home, unemployment or idleness, or just a desire to chart own destinies?

"Over the years I have learned my lessons very well
Lesson one: everyone is a bird and has a nest
Lesson two: most birds fly and so must we
Lesson three: we all go away some time to rest
From the routine"

A nest is a place of birth, of every bird thus making home also a place of birth for people. Africa is home no matter where one is born at in the continent, where we only fly out of to reach our destinies and, come back after touring other places as residents or mere workers.

The voice in Lazarus Sauti's poem Simuka, instructs mother Africa to stand up and protect her resources from plundering by foreigners as it encourages Africa to make her children the heirs to her heritage.

"Africa,
Simukauonekere.
Mira panzvimbo vana vawane pekubata
Simuka uchengetedze nhaka yevana, Africa!"

45

Here Africa who is the mother of children is urged to keep safe her children's heritage. Mothers are the managers and keepers of home as affirmed by our proverb which says 'musha mukadzi' for a home to be a home it is because of the presence of a WOMAN. Without a woman, there is no home. Mothers take care of their children's health through their cooking of nutritious foods in the home.

Talking to a colleague, about the book by Batsirai Chigama, Chidora said, the voices collected in Chigama's collection are a reflection of the period under interrogation which even led to the Operation Restore Legacy of home, a military intervention that brought in the new administration in November 2017.

A voice in Memory Chirere's poem 'Pamhararano' (crossroads) from his debut Shona poetry collection, 'Bhuku Risina Basa: Nekuti Rakanyorwa Masikati' asks everyone talking ill about home that if all those that are clapping hands for the voice are silent, what else will the voice talk about?

"Kana vose vanondiomberera vanyarara
vave kuda kunzwa zvimwe zvine musoro
ndichataurei?"

The voice further asks that if the poem that the voice is reciting, reading or writing has exposed all the bad about home, and made the voice the hero of exposing the ills about home, where else can it go and stay?

"Kana detembo rino rafumura nyika
ndave gamba rokunongedza zvitadzo
ndichaenda kupi?"

The voice in the poem continues to introspect and point that home is where one was born in and the umbilical cord was interred.

Gather the Children is not a single voice but a collective in a dialogue with other voices produced before it which also were not happy with the state of affairs in the homeland whether perceived in the mind or in the physical or the spiritual. The poets dream and hope for a home of peace, unity and understanding though they differ on what home is but all agree on that wherever home is it should be a place of happiness.

References

Audrey Lindani Mutinhiri, Edmond Shonhiwa and Noreen Sadziwa, *Flowers of the Dry Season* (Forteworx Press, 2015)

Batsirai Chigama, *gather the children*, (Ntombekhaya, 2018)

Brian Chikwava, *Harare North* (Jonathan Cape, 2009)

Charles Mungoshi and Ignatius Mabasa, *Illuminations 25* (The Rathasker press, 2009)

David Mungoshi, Live Like an Artist, (Bhabhu Books, 2017)

Lazarus Sauti, *Nei?* (Royal Books, 2017)

Lilian Dube and Mgcini Nyoni, *Daybreak* (Poetry Bulawayo, 2010)

Memory Chirere, Bhuku Risina Basa:Nekuti Rakanyorwa Masikati, (Bhabhu Books, 2015)

FALLACY OF THE OPPOSITION MDC AND DEMOCRACY IN ZIMBABWE

Tendai Rinos Mwanaka

The MDC doesn't have a soul (propulsion ideology) other than opposing ZANU-PF, in actual fact there is nothing that really connects people to its ideology other than the overused human rights, constitution and rule of law noises. Please note I am not saying these aren't important, they are, with a soul that connects all these to the people. People in the MDC fight against ZANUPF because of bread and butter issues, but they also forget we have an educated or continuously trying to educate themselves, electorate in Zimbabwe. The people have been exposed to all sorts of knowledges from all over the world; their mind needs to be fed too. That's why poor countries like Afghanistan have these great philosophical/religious ideologies connected to their politics that they are willing to fight for, not just food. ZANUPF has always been a party of ideologies, some well-thought, some not implementable, but they use these to fight against their failure to provide the basics to the electorate, for example ideas of economic emancipation that go beyond food like land distribution, industry indigenization(one of the bad policies), national ideologies like the Bira celebrations, Independence and Heroes celebrations, and have made national events seem like they are ZANUPF ideologies or things, and the MDC have nothing to counteract these.

The next issue that lacks in MDC is strategic intent and vision. The vision should work hand and in hand with ideology outlined above. In Africa there are visions that are too superfluous and western-centric to the electorate. Human rights, constitutionalism etc… are some of these when you fail to locate them within issues to do with African humanness- *ubuntuism*, respect, community, ownership. And coupled to Nelson Chamisa's last election vision of spaghetti roads and village airports, imagine a country that is 60 percent rural and you are focusing on issues solely western-centric like human rights, spaghetti roads, village airports and when the electorate checks the roads- they are broken beyond belief- how can one dream, over-dream, or day dream to cover the chasm between vision and reality. A vision should be ambitious and sound achievable too, within a foreseeable lifetime. Seriously you can't ask humanity to bank on something that might happen in 50-100 yrs. Humans are selfish and adaptive at most- it has to happen to me or to my kids for me to be more inspired by it. The MDC talk big and *hubridiotic* stuff but there is no mechanisms and implementation strategy that is put into place to win the elections especially in the rural areas. Every election period they barely hit the ground yet the ZANUPF never stops campaigning- is always on the ground especially since the economic mess-ups of pre-2008 almost accosted the ZANUPF the stick to the MDC. The strategic intent to win the elections has always been MDC Achilles heels because there is always a big chasm between their reality and their vision.

The MDC doesn't even field election agents on election day in rural constituencies (50 plus constituencies in 2018) and how can a party that fails to guarantee its voters rights to vote without fear or harm be able to really go out there in the rural areas and win the hearts and minds of more voters. The MDC thinks just because people are fed up with ZANUPF and every time they fail to win they accuse ZANUPF of stealing as if MDC is automatically entitled to win because ZANUPF has failed. But ZANUPF focus on important areas, the rural vote and win that vote.

People in the rural areas have different conception of what a country means versus to those in the cities and how to measure effectiveness of the leaders. ZANUPF is still getting 67percent of MPs mostly in the rural areas and there is little dispute from the MDC about that, it shows that ZANUPF still has the heart of the electorate in the rural areas- they might not like the president in some cases, but no doubt they still view the ZANUPF favorably…the president still benefits from this love and its asking a lot from the MDC's president to win the election when they can't even deny the ZANUPF two thirds parliamentary seats.

MDC has overbanked on the noise of the urban electorate, more especially on the foreign based Zimbabweans' noise and think that just because there is so much anger in the social Medias and newspapers that would translate into votes. NO. As long as the foreign vote is not allowed they can make all the noise they could and still lose. As long as millions of youths in urban areas make noise on the social Medias and never register to vote (which is the case in urban areas). The youths only begin to vote in Zimbabwe way later when there are in their 30s. Most of the youths in their twenties, or late teens are not registered to vote, and are not interested in political issues. There is nothing that translates the noise they might make into votes. This is the problem that MDC's western handlers (US, EU etc) fail to understand.

MDC has not shaken its shameful (to the chunk of the electorate) connection to western donors (which that good chunk of the country also feel have had strong hand in our problems). The dispute with the western nations started with the land issue, which the western donors took the side of the white farmer and punished Zimbabweans over this. The land is in the hands of Zimbabweans and it was an internal issue, some Zimbabweans who got the land have used the land to change their circumstances and some have failed but still have rights to the land, and its asking a lot from the voters to hate ZANUPF that gave them land that the whites were refusing with, which the western nations punished the country over through the sanctions. A country has no iron borders within, whereby you can say *oh this sanction is targeted on A, and will never affect B or C, or D*, when there is continuous linkages between A, B, C, D.... it's a stupid western argument that sanctions were targeted sanctions as if you have removed those targeted from the country and they are living their own lives away from those untargeted. I will deal with the sanction issue separately. It's precisely because of the Land issue that the West put the country under sanctions, not the now over-emphasized human rights issue (what of Kenya that kills more of its people during elections than Zimbabwe, where are the human rights sanctions, what of the tens of thousands white farmers murdered in South African farms every year (are they not humans or it's because they still own the land), what of the hundreds of Nigerians that die in their elections), does it mean the electorate in Zimbabwe is more dear to the West... The MDC people are more interested in western donor money than democracy, I will tackle this party's democracy and constitutionalism to prove this, you get the feeling the electorate in Zimbabwe that tolerate the western ideas do so for the buck but still a lot stick with ZANUPF at the ballot boxes.

Stealing the elections is another card the MDC have overused. So if elections are always stolen, according to the MDC, why bother voting, the electorate has come to this position point in Zimbabwe. Why waste time. MDC focuses on silly examples of how elections are rigged and never come to the table with something definitive to impress the electorate on how ZANUPF rig elections. Check the 2018 elections and the noise they made and yet when they were asked for proof by the Supreme Court, they had nothing other than theories and fumbled up numbers, as I noted before they didn't even have elections agents in 50 constituencies they were disputing the vote. Instead of seeing a half full glass by pushing to win the election so that the glass will be full and thus make people have faith in the system, I am always told what I am trying to do to correct the problem will never yield the result and thus I am made to settle for a half empty glass, and do nothing. This narrative of victims mentality needs to change or we will continue wasting our time doing these elections that the MDC will reject as long as they don't win, wasting our lives in an intractable fight by keeping asking others to try to sort of our situations and thus making them worsen than they were. Since 2000, it's hard to point on the progress we have made other than nebulous things like democracy, human rights, constitutionalism etc… We are poor; poorer than we were in 1959, the MDC says since 1923…, so tell me how one would expect the electorate to continue with this fight when he is dying from hunger, from malnutrition, from lack of a horizon to grow…there is such a thing as too much. We need to refocus the struggle issue and make a new trajectory that cares about the voter more than the voted for.

This has caused us to look around the world and try to see if this democracy we have been fighting for is the only way to grow. No it is not. There is a lot of beauty you would find in countries that are far behind us democratically but have made huge stride in providing for their citizens than we have made with our democracy wars in the last 20 years…look at the likes of Rwanda, Malaysia, Singapore, China etc…most of these countries were poor than Zimbabwe in 1980, and yet some of these countries have moved from developing into developed countries and have raised millions out of poverty without practicing democracy, at least not the textbook kind of democracy Zimbabwe is bent on. A benevolent dictator or leader is finding ground in the electorate's minds and heart in Zimbabwe, even in the whole of Africa than is democracy, the western clean kind of democracy we read in the books and try to emulate. But no western nation is really practicing this kind of democracy. We have suffered all our lives and nothing seems to be coming from the MDC and the democratic fights, thus a lot of the electorate are beginning to find ZANUPF mantra of economic development more interesting

The MDC leadership problem is the most glaring of its weaknesses. I advocated in *Zimbabwe: The Urgency of Now*, for the whole opposition body to unite together for the 2013 elections, and eventually they did before the 2018 elections. But it's one thing to unite and another thing to unite under the right leadership. Before they could really unite, the MDC president Morgan Tsvangirai died and left his party, MDC-T hang in leadership struggle he had created. Overally since its formation in 1999, the MDC never really resolved its leadership problems to show the kind of democracy they wished we had that the ZANUPF wasn't offering us. The MDC constitution states categorically that a leader only serves at a position for two terms, thus Tsvangirai's term of office should have come to pass in 2007, before the 2008 election but the party ignored that and installed Tsvangirai into a lifetime of some sort presidency. They enthused you can't change a general in the middle of a war. Where we in a war. What about the constitutionalism it preaches at every drop of a hat, what of democracy. The MDC didn't resolve the leadership problem even after the GNU, and thus it broke up further with Tendai Biti and Elton Mangoma (sec gen and treasurer) outing of the MDCT and this was the second breakdown of the MDC after the 2005 schism that saw Welshman Ncube and company leaving after disputing the senator participation vote which Tsvangirai had overrode the NEC executive decision by imposing his view, and refused the party participation, even though the majority had voted for participation in the 2005 Senate elections. This new break up by Tendai Biti and Elton Mangoma saddled the party with a murky leadership top. Tsvangirai was allowed to abuse power by electing, against the constitution of the MDC, two extra vice presidents in Nelson Chamisa and Elias Mudzuri.

Why he did that is still everyone's wild guess. I will narrow it down to that Thokozana Khupe, Douglas Mwonzora, Lovemore Moyo (as vice president, secretary general and national chairman respectively) posed threat to his power as the president. His top leadership were not happy with him continuing, knowing he was indecisive and wont on dictatorial tendencies, and so those were making moves to dump him, and to counter their moves, he promoted two of his dumped friends (Nelson Chamisa and Elias Mudzuri) to crowd the top leadership and make them jostle each other than focusing on him. He learned this game from Mugabe. Mugabe when faced with unrest in his party would create something to harness the energies of those plotting against him, usually by bringing back a disgraced leader and put him or her in the middle, for example Jonathan Moyo at one time. It means the top leadership would focus on each other, trying to upstage each other instead of focusing on him.

Nelson Chamisa was dumped by the MDC electorate through Tsvangirai's influence in the MDC 2014 elections when he had aligned the whole party towards voting for him for the secretary general position. Tsvangirai knowing the threat and kind of power Chamisa had created towards the 2014 MDC elections, counteracted that by pushing the party delegates to vote for Mwonzora on the sec general position.

For how can one explain why someone who had gotten a single endorsement over someone who had gotten the rest of the endorsements would upstage this one already endorsed, without someone very powerful in leadership circles stemming the tide? As for Mudzuri he had been recalled by Tsvangirai from the GNU ministerial portfolio after poor performance, back into some shoddy secretariat in the party. So these two were taken from the MDC dustbin right back to the top 3, unconstitutionally, to protect himself from or to counter Khupe, Mwonzora, Lovemore Moyo and Abednico Ncube's threat to his presidency. As a white flag, he said he promoted those to help him, but that's precisely the job of the vice presidency (Khupe) - and when he died there was confusion as to who was the rightful heir. Chamisa, the cunning politician he is exploited the party levers and groups to upstage the other two VPs, Mudzuri and Khupe, using insults, threats, beatings, threats of arson (the youths almost burned alive Khupe and Mwonzora in Buhera during Tsvangirai's burial rites), thus he roughshod over the party's constitution that was explicit that only the VP elected at congress by the people has the right to take over from the president(Khupe here), and that no other body is allowed to elect the presidency outside congress. The party would only elect a full presidency at congress. But Chamisa used the MDC National Executive Council to impose himself and help with the control of the party leadership, thus he came to power unconstitutionally just like Tsvangirai had stayed in power unconstitutionally.

Was he the right candidate for the party, the majority felt he was so they kept a blind eye on the unconstitutionality happening, fought those who tried to suggest otherwise. These faithfuls knew if they had followed the constitution and installed Khupe, it meant Khupe was going to be the face of the party in 2018 elections and afterwards until a congress was held months later. Which, in itself, was going to be a chaotic event knowing the likes of Mwonzora were already eyeing for the presidency after doing well as sec general. It was going to be difficult to remove a settled in Khupe, let alone to vest in Chamisa. The other explanation is she is a woman and Zimbabwe, frankly speaking, is a chauvinistic society and women leaders are still one hell of salt to fresh wounds of many men in Zimbabwe, let alone to the woman themselves... Funnily enough women in Zimbabwe don't really believe a fellow woman can be a good leader. Sorry for this sweeping statement, but I stand corrected. They imposed Chamisa immediately for the future.

Was he the right candidate, at least for me who has voted MDC since 1999? It's a big fat *Hell No*. I would have settled for Mwonzora, Khupe Mudzuri, or Moyo. But critically I would have settled for Mwonzora. He was the best leader they had after Biti and Welshamn left to succeed Tsvangirai. He had the full respect of the party supporters and MDC executive (Note here I am not talking of voters) and he had beaten Chamisa in the 2014 election (I say that reluctantly) to the secretary general post, beating someone who had all but won it. Chamisa, over the years has shown he is never interested in an election that he doesn't control and manipulate to win. Even the later congress for the MDCA Alliance, the party created to avoid the MDC-T power struggle lawsuits was riven by manipulations. He controlled everything, was part of the organs running the election in which he was contesting, the election was run in the middle of the night, he disbarred and kicked out provincial leadership that wasn't supporting him and his choices of candidates, and cleared out those who wanted Mwonzora or Khupe, controlled the party's mouth pieces both in the party and in general media such that the traditional supporters of the MDC who preferred Mwonzora were denied the right to determine their destiny. He used the party organs including youths to threaten Mwonzora left and right, calling him names just for raising his hand to contest a party position in the so-called democratic institution, MDC, and cajoled Mwonzora to give him wide birth for Manicaland province, and he would support Mwonzora for sec general position. Note Manicaland only endorsed Chamisa when Mwonzora had folded his towel and backed Chamisa.

There was the likelihood of the previous congress, the 2014 congress repeating itself again, had Mwonzora stuck to his guns and get Manicaland endorsement and locked horns with Chamisa for presidency, all things equal…but Mwonzoera knew he had lost his supporters in the other provinces as Chamisa used party organs to clean out Mwonzora's supporters before congress. All these were happening in a party that prides itself of being constitutional, democratic etc..

Why do I still insist No to Chamisa as the right candidate for the MDC? Chamisa basically is a tactical leader. The dog you sent out to bite up and scare competition, not the dog that sits pretty and cool until the little backing Chihuahuas have petered down. He has always been the tactical leader even in student politics, MDC youth structures, as MDC's organizing secretary (the sec who does the grunt level work, the one who follows instruction from the top). For me those are the suitable positions for Chamisa. He was never the strategist who has the larger story, overview, or vision. So on the top of the MDC we have a leader who has no strategic and visionary acumen. The same analysis applies to Biti, he is a barking dog too. Even back when he got a strategic position as MDC secretary general (from the reports we heard in news medias he messed up that as he focused on barking instead of righting party structures such that by 2013 the party was so messy, had no finances for elections and he later left with party properties and finances to build his own splinter party). It was Mwonzora who cleaned that up. Then on the top MDC Alliance structures we also have Welshman Ncube who personally thinks he is the strategist for the party…but does he have the voice to be heard? Knowing he comes from Matabeleland province, a province he doesn't even seem to have a handle on. Has he proven he is a strategist during his stint with the MDC before 2005 split, and his own brand of the MDC after?

He left the MDC in 2005 over a dispute with Tsvangirai and the MDC on the senate election. As I have noted before he favoured participation to stay relevant, yet Tsvangirai's camp favoured boycott over waste of resources. But was that enough to pack your bags and go…that's what a strategist asks before giving up. In his brand of the MDC he promoted Arthur Mutambara, a robotics professor to lead the party because he felt he himself had no power to entice the predominantly Shona electorate needed to win an election. Yes this is tribal, but at the basic level was Arthur the best he could get to lead him. Arthur behaved exactly like a robot during his stint as president of MDC-N, a Welshaman Ncube controlled robot … and sometimes Mugabe got the hang of that robot and controlled it, sometimes it was Tsvangirai who got his hands on the mouse of the computer that controlled the robot. My question is, or my answer is if you say you are a strategic leader, then you prefer putting tactical people ahead of you, every time…there is something wrong with your position and analogue. Here, it wasn't even a strategic gimmick, because there was no chance whatsoever that Arthur or Welshman would win the biggest chunk of the electorate and takeover. Eventually the robotics professor went back to school and Welshman found his way back into the bigger MDC tent to start new machinations. All in all the top 3 in the MDCA position is filled by tactical thinkers and leaders. And its even worse as you go down the party levers: Job Sikhala barks more than anyone in Zimbabwe, so are Calton Hwende, Fadzai Mahere, Thabita Khumalo etc) they are all tactical thinkers, maybe the exception is the woman third vice president. This is what happens when the tactical thinkers are given full reign, they control everything by extruding the strategic thinkers because they are used to working with dirty tactics to stifle any dissent; the stable strategic handlers were extruded with Mwonzora and Mudzuri.

Years after the 2018 election, we are in the 3rd year towarding to the 2023 election, they are still barking and whinnying about the stolen 2018 election instead of strategizing around 2023. So who, you can ask. Because now we have two MDCs, each saying they are the right MDC, one run by Chamisa, and the other by Mwonzora (who took over after disposing off Khupe, the acting MDC president in a shoddy congress, replicating Chamisa's congress.). As an electorate in such confusing and chaotic opposition minefield you want to see these leaders banding together for the bigger purpose, really this is not the time to be arguing about who has a bigger penis, but no Chamisa and Mwonzora are still fighting about who has the bigger dick, so are their supporters. Chamisa was overtaken by the events of his unconstitutionality; Mwonzora doesn't inspire confidence to the die-hard young MDC camp. We are left with one and half years to the 2023 poll and there is nothing tangible, no roadmap to wining the seats back from ZANUPF. I am sure what the MDCA is focusing on is how many seats they will get versus how many the MDCT will, its Mwonzoro vs Chamisa's egos that will play out. I am sure in the beginning of this essay I was talking of Mwonzora, not Khupe, and you wondered why? The fight has always been between Mwonzora and Chamisa…this is the fight that played out, and is still playing. No tactical runners are in the rural areas because they are at the presidency, barking at each other. We are heading toward another election the MDC can only lose. It's a waste.

The MDC's top leadership are increasingly becoming obvious have never been interested in serving the people it purports to serve, but are fighting for positions on the feeding lots. They would make a bit of noise, stage poorly organized protests to hoodwink the donors, throw a few poor people to the wolves (ZANUPF controlled police and army here) and our stupid security establishment is caught with their trousers on the knees after beating up these few protestors, and the MDC will cry pell-mell over the donors medias, get a few bucks and become quiet as they fest until they are broke again and start on another donor attention grabbing gimmick, get the loot, spend it and go back to the streets again. There is now no wholesale movement towards fighting

ZANUPF'S hegemony in its battle grounds. The MDC leaders are parasitic mercenaries and the electorate is left dry and hanging, every time

We need a third force, an alternative party, an alternative consensus that appeals across both divides, ZANUPF and MDC. We need a third force rooted in the middle, interested in serving the people, Zimbabwe…not parties, not people, not vested interests, not tribal adhesions and hangovers that both ZANUPF and MDC are wont on.

As I noted MDC can only lose 2023. To start with it is always running late to the events unfolding in Zimbabwe. It has already lost 3 years moaning about losing the 2018 election, which if they had any strategic thinkers among them, these could have told the likes of Chamisa to move on 6 months after the election, or just after losing the appeal to the Supreme Court. If you are wise enough you won't be expecting to win anything after the last law body has decided against you. It's clear to anyone with a little bit of sense that the MDC didn't do enough to win 2018, let alone to guarantee the safety of the vote, and its idiotic to expect the last court of the land to wade into political territory to gift a party over another. Anyone who understands separation of powers of the levers of government would understand it was never going to happen. To disregard an election over little or no evidence is for the court to wade into politics, to usurp the functions of other levers of government and the country will suffer from constitutional crisis rendering it ungovernable. In simple terms the MDC failed to prove ZANUPF had stolen the vote…you can allege someone has done this or that, but without proof or evidence, it's just an unfounded accusation. This is the basics of law. They couldn't event present their own V11 forms because they hadn't fielded enough monitors, or they were reckless, or deep down they knew they had no hard evidence so they resorted on twisting the Latinity in the law and make a lot of noise, just to tarnish the election. It was their own duty to have their forms, not ZEC or ZANUPF, not the courts. As I noted I don't see the MDC wining 2023 because to start with they never focus on the right issue at the right time.

As we marched toward the 2018 election, any wise strategist would have advised them they had no chance with the 2018 presidential vote. It takes time to build a leader who would stay the test of time. Chamisa was in office for less than half a year, and had even at that come to power through a polarizing process that weakened its structures and frayed the MDC power base. I have voted for the MDC for all its existence but I wouldn't have voted for Chamisa in 2018 if I was in the country. I was angry with the way he had shit over everything to come to power. Before Tsvangirai was even buried he had started power mongering games which really goes against Ubuntu values. I am not just interested in removing ZANUPF from power. I am interested in entrenching democratic values for the future generations and now I don't see the difference between MDC and ZANUPF. But ZANUPF is always trying to deceitfully portray themselves in better light and they are serious moves by ZANUPF to gobble up that middle space I noted we need a third force for.

With the land reform and Mugabe's leadership survival games the ZANUPF became far right, radically approaching the land reform, indigenization, the wrecking fights with the West over neocolonialism and sovereignty, the MDC were somewhere in the centre to centre left on our political swing and they got a lot of support from the growing educated middle class and the poor class. But ZANUPF, under Mnangangwa is moving towards the centre, even sometimes pushing to the centre and centre left thereby squeezing the MDC to the left, which is a very tight space in a conservative country like Zimbabwe. The only way the MDC can win the elections in Zimbabwe is to push back to the centre and be the heaven of all forces that distrusts ZANUPF, and the centre of a country is where the largest majority are, in the present day Zimbabwe it's the rural vote. They have to unequivocally accept some of the things ZANUPF do to win the rural vote like land reform and push these things off ZANUPF's election basket by making them a national thing not party things. That would mean winning off its white supporters and donors, but it is exactly these donors that have killed the MDC by pushing it to the radical left and west-centric.

The hardest lesson the MDC has to learn now is to have the new boys graduate from being boys into being men, girls into women. They have to learn how to grow its newfound support, close to 1 000 000 new votes to propel them into power in 2023. In *Zimbabwe: The Urgency of Now*, I noted the MDC has been losing the election with pretty the same margin since 2008 and the reason is because of *Us*, its boys and girls back in post-2000 Zimbabwe who had left the country and never returned after the 2008 election. It had not got the time and spaces to build back that base by 2013. But the younger brothers we had left when we went overseas became grown up boys, our kids we left home as we went abroad to earn a living to take care of them hated ZANUPF as much as we did and by 2018 these were the new voters who pushed Chamisa into 2mill plus votes, which Tsvangirai last did in 2008. And it is these boys and girls, on one side I am alluding to. They have to keep these boys and add more before 2023, which is an impossible order as a lot of these new voters might leave before 2023.

On the other spectrum the boys are Chamisa and his leadership cahoots. They were left with a good party, its upto them to grow up to become men and women they ought to be.

Continuing with why I think it wasn't strategic for the MDC to focus all its resources in 2018 on the presidential vote. They should have tried to win the parliamentary vote, push back the ZANUPF off the two thirds majority stage, win enough seats to make it impossible for ZANUPF to do anything in Zimbabwe. The most exciting thing about Zimbabwe in 2008 was the wrestling away from the ZANUPF of Zimbabwe's parliament by Tsvangirai's MDC. In actual fact this is where the powers are. They are the ones who make the laws, who debate the constitution, who can take the president to task. Winning the president without the parliamentary vote was naïve on the part of the MDC. How can you run a country like Zimbabwe without control of the lower levers of power. Even in 2008, and post that, it was difficult for Tsvangirai to get things done, even with majority Mps, what of with just one fifth that the MDC got. With a healthy parliamentary vote we will be set for a good show on 2023 presidential vote. Now ZANUPF has two thirds majority and has been tinkering with the constitution, entrenching their interests with at one time 27 amendments …and these would pass with a two thirds majority it has. Now winning 2023 is an impossible horizon. And this is one instance they focused on the wrong fight and came to the decisional table when it was too late.

When I started writing this essay as you might have realized the MDC was still intact even though they were fighting, now they have broken and fragmented badly into two camps opposing each other as MDCT and MDCA, this after the Supreme court judgment of March 2020 that illegalized Chamisa's ascendency to power as unconstitutional. This happened after a card-carrying Gokwe north MDC member took the party to court.. whilst a lot of people if they had read this essay before the latest schism would have disagreed with me that Chamisa and his deputies are not strategic thinkers, but after the way they handled the succession issue, especially after the supreme court judgment, I think a lot can agree with me now. Chamisa missed so many chances to seal the rift and kept to his intransigency as he preached and preached, never taking a position to seal the rift or move on. He left the whole thing to pan out the way it did. He had no wet towel to douse the fires and the fires consumed him and the party. He kept making so many accusations against ZANUPF even though the drama was playing out inside the MDC, he blamed everyone else, and his supporters blamed everyone else with their *Chamisa chete chete* slogans. He is still playing the victim's game that Tsvangirai perfected and this cult of leadership has left the MDC in the open. ZANUPF has moved away from *Mugabe chete chete* mantra, at least not as publicly as they used to do. Mnangagwa's speech a few months ago shows that's where he is driving the party towards when he said the days of the spectre of leadership died with Mugabe. It needs to die too in the MDC, or just being publicly shunned in the party.

PS: we can still read this essay to mean MDC is now the new party, CCC….it's still the same people and issues. It's just a name change, just like movement from MDC, to MDCT, to MDCA, now it's CCC

Eppel explores 'unbelonging' in new work: Between the Lines
Beniah Munengwa

To be a person who lived on the other side of the fence always leaves one with a problem of binaries. One such man is John Eppel, a writer who finds himself in a category which fits many, the likes of David Coltart and Doris Lessing, who, however, find themselves belonging to neither side of the "racial" fence.

Just like Coltart, Eppel at one time found himself fighting on the side of the white man's forces. Afterwards, we locate these two figures attempting to shed off those shackles of racist and imperialist terms to being the eye that explores and cautions both good and bad in either racial grouping.

In them, we find a quest of belonging and an attempt to fit in, into African humanity with every inch of their bone and not be seen as savages, as reverse racism now puts it.

The content of Eppel's writing is that of a man who is in touch with the problems of either civilisation. He is a writer, who in an interview with Ambrose Musiyiwa, claimed to have been strongly influenced by Charles Dickens' focus on the marginalised people and he, himself, too has been marginalised, having had many of his manuscripts rejected by Zimbabwean publishing houses.

One of the works that relate to his claim of being overtly African is his latest offering, *White Man Walking*. The name White Man Walking is, however, not new, having been used by American writer, Ward Brehm, for the book, White Man Walking: An American Businessman's Spiritual Adventure in Africa.

In the new offering, Eppel explores the nuances of colonial and post-colonial existence in Zimbabwe. Some major recurring thematic concerns dealt with are the closeness to violence that the government is, when dealing with anyone who seems to go against it.

One notable feature is that all stories were written while former President Robert Mugabe was still in power. The story, Democracy at Work and at Play, underscores the deep-rootedness of Mugabeism, especially in rural communities. While the constitution-making process was supposed to be puritanical, the lack of accommodation of divergent thought and the underscored vision of trying to convert the Constitution into another version of craft that extends Mugabe's time in office takes charge.

Eppel, in an independent interview, highlighted: "My main concern in my prose is to ridicule greed, cruelty, self-righteousness and related vices like racism, sexism, jingoism, and homophobia."

With regard to his revelation, much of his stories pick up the strands that influence the way in which Zimbabwean governance and leadership unfolded.

He explains why he prefers to use satire in his writing saying: "I am under no illusion that my satires will make the slightest bit of difference, but nobody, not even those who are ashamed of nothing, likes to be laughed at."

Chiefly among Eppel's subjects of satire is the greed associated with the politician or his wife. Symbolising it was the recurrent question, "Where's my tub of Kentucky fries?"

In the short story, The Award Ceremony, instead of mourning the dead after a tragedy, the minister's obese wife finds herself only caring about her Kentucky fries.

On a deeper look, the way the politician's wife causes the suffering of innocent civilians and without feeling a sense of shame is synonymous with the bad girl tag associated with the then First Lady, Grace Mugabe.

In the era of Mugabeism, the probability that anybody would be working for the Central Intelligence Organisation was very high.

Such is the case of Mr Abednego Dolobenj, a school teacher in the story, Profile of a School Teacher.

The outstanding story for me is NGO Games, primarily because it explores the template formulae in which non-governmental organisations go through in their day-to- day running. Blended with deep-set humour, Eppel portrays NGOs as organisations that thrive mainly on report writing and generation and less of any helpful initiatives.

This story falls under the same category as the author and poet's thoughts, that "international organisations will not help a white artist, no matter how poor," he is.

While the overall picture may portray Eppel's satire as overtly pointed to the system heads, one cannot ignore that some of it is pointed at the general public, who foolishly assume that they can unearth the roots of the system single-handedly. The end result, as shown in the stories, The Weight Loser and Sewage Pipe, where characters attempt to demonstrate against the system and end up molested by people on the lower end of the system.

Eppel's book stands as an independent project that is outstanding and refreshing on a different level, thanks to the meticulous input of the publisher. Thus in spite of a few errors, it is a book that I can proudly add onto my library.

This article was originally published in the NewsDay Issue of, 11, June 2019.

Title: White Man Walking
Author: John Eppel
Publisher: Mwanaka Media and Publishing (2018)
ISBN: 978-0-7974-9548-7

Screw the Zimbabwean!

Tendai Rinos Mwanaka

From far off memory the story of Zimbabwe or Zimbabweans has been of screwing and being screwed. We love being screwed. We screw each other. If you like screwing please go to Zimbabwe. Here, it's a Zimbabwe of both black and white. The Shona people screwed the Khoi people off their land, then the Shona were screwed by the Ndebele, the Ndebele and Shona were screwed by the Whites, and these returned the favour, screwed the Whites. Blacks screwed Whites, Whites screwed Blacks, throw in the Indians, Chinese, Coloureds etc …it's a *screwing screw, screw screw zhiim zhiim pot*. It's the sounds of the screws and drill machine, filling every hole it is holeing into. Mugabe screwed the Zimbabweans for over 37 years, and we allowed him to screw us as we moaned with pleasure. *Ummm, aaaah, ishsss….,* Please note Zimbabweans love being screwed so don't mistake the noise they make when they are being screwed by their politicians as pain. No, it's pleasure! When Mugabe was done screwing the Zimbos, he left it to his protégé to continue screwing them. Hear them now as they moan! *"There is no food", "There is no fuel", "There is no electricity", "There is no water", "There is no foreign currency", "There is not enough school fees", "There is no transport", "There are no jobs", "There is no industry", "There is no president", "There is no hope", "There is no this", "There is no that and those ones"* Even you can hear the mournful sounds in these noises. They are actually enjoying being screwed. They allowed for that. When you think you know so much, and the Zimbabweans boast about being the most educated people in Africa- I am sure you have heard of this noise- in actual fact you don't know a thing. You should be learning. You should be growing. You should be adapting. Tell me why would a people who hated what Robert did to them for 37 years, would allow the same screwer to get away with all that he stole, all the sadness and pain he visited upon them. They all agreed to leave Robert alone and let him rest. I am sure the old screwer still chuckles at the Zimbabweans with unbelief at how he got away with all that! If he was that bad he should be rotting in jail. Screw human dignity, where is the human dignity for the millions he screwed for a lifetime, screw mercies and the we-are-the-most-civilized-people-on-the-continent self-hypnosis, screw the Zimbabweans and their civilized poverty of mind and existence! This would have served as a reminder to Mnangagwa that if he screws us he will eventually face the same screws, but no, we didn't. Now Mnangagwa is happily screwing us left, right and centre and we are enjoying it. Sideways, backwards, in the mouth, every hole is filled up as the crocodile drills us. And mark my words, the next in line will come and screw us. You can go and debate who you think is the next in line but for sure he will screw us, whether it's the, *it will work*, soldier... Note: yes it will work in screwing us, or whether it's the little boycrazywarhead power gloat, screwbag of opposition politics. He so loves moaning about how Mnangagwa is screwing us whilst he is screwing us himself. So to you African brother and sister out there when you see a Zimbabwean, know that he is screwier screwable. Try to screw him. South Africa, I didn't say do xenophobia on him, just screw him. You are asking me how? It's very simple, just screw his malleable mind. And he will never let go of you! You American, Russian, Indian, Chinese, European, Asian... come to the African tropical paradise of screwing and enjoy yourself. And I tell you, the Zimbabwean will be so grateful for the screwing!

Confessions of a book reviewer and writer
Tanaka Chidora

Introduction

For almost two years now, I have been reviewing literary texts for *The Herald* (Zimbabwe's largest daily) and my own blog (www.litmindssite.wordpress.com). It's been a mixed experience for me which involved hunting down books whose authors were as elusive as the mythical Eldorado; or sometimes receiving poorly converted PDF versions of the authors' "latest" publications. For a reviewer living in Zimbabwe, buying a review copy every week whose cost was superior to what I would get for the review was an untenable choice. Then there was always this other book, from a zealous and self-published author (or one who had published with a publishing house that was set up specifically to publish that particular book) with missing words, a clichéd plot, an acquired taste… generally, a boring, half-done (sometimes quarter-done) read! My experiences as a reviewer have shown me that the future cannot be bright. I know the reading culture is in some ICU, but writers are also doing themselves a lot of disservice by not writing well, or by making their books difficult to get. This paper is therefore a laissez-faire collection of reflections based on my 2-year stint in book-reviewing circles. The general conclusion from these reflections is that marketing, editing and creativity need to be revamped for books to leave footprints even in this era where readers must be coaxed to actually read books.

Uncle Tich, Books and I

I grew up in the village with my parents and my siblings (Sue, Josy, Anne and, later towards the 2000s, Tawa). I was born in the 80s and started going to school in 1992. For my generation, especially those who grew up in the village, there was no pre-school. You just reached school-going age (7 years) without any pre-Grade One nurturing. Pre-school was merely a matter of going to the community centre (this one under the Musasa Tree, near the township) and eating porridge, this a product of some philanthropic interventions to make sure that village children did not succumb to kwashiorkor, whatever that was. By the way, going to school was also a matter of being able to touch your ear by stretching your hand above the dome of your head. Being able to pronounce 'Birth Certificate' was an added advantage. The rest was left to your Grade One teachers who really did a good job of making you pronounce the 26 letters of the alphabet by using a song about *manhanga* (pumpkins). I had a problem with the letter 'K', a problem that lasted a couple of months. I breezed through my Grade One without being able to read my school report. I would get to know my class position after getting home. Then my mother's facial expression would tell me if the report contained good news or not. It always contained good news.

My first free reading involved the book of Chronicles, which, in Shona translates to *Makoronike*. The Shona bible of old represented a reading hiccup for a naïve reader of my calibre, so the funny 'zv' and 'ch' in there provided a couple of hilarious moments for my mother who loved to eavesdrop on my reading.[1]

From Grade One to university, my parents, God bless them, trusted my work ethic so much that they practically left the choice of what to read, and when to read, to me. I don't remember them tyrannically dictating the homework-first-TV later rule to me that I see many kids enduring today. Of course, you might want to say TVs were not a common phenomenon in the village in those days. So find anything to use instead of TV. *Mahwani Touch*, bakery or *tsoro* if

---

[1] For 'zv', the old Shona bible only provided a funny looking sagging 'z', and for 'ch' there was only a lonely looking 'c'.

you want. Our parents practised a laissez-faire approach to education: I had to decide what I loved, and they had to provide the means (sometimes labouriously). Lots of times, I had to join them, either as father's *dhakaboy* (a colloquial term for someone who mixes mortar for the builder), or as mother's runner at the township market. During the cropping season, after helping in the fields, I had to look after our small herd of cattle. With such a busy schedule, novels still managed to find me. Of course, reading at the pastures was a traumatic experience, for the books that is. Many of them had mud splotches and dog ears to show off the experience of being read at the pastures.

By the time I completed my seventh grade at Mutya Primary School, I had already breezed my way through every popular Shona novel one could think of. My reading of these novels was necessitated by two things. First, Josy loved to unceremoniously insert long paragraphs of any Shona novel she would be reading at any given time into an everyday conversation. Imagine, you are having a conversation about invading Mbuya VaRusekeni's mango orchard, and Josy rattles up something from *Kutonhodzwa KwaChauruka* for effect. Only a perfect WhatsApp emoji can capture the confusion that would appear on our faces. So I took to reading every Shona novel that came my way. Some came as complete packages; others came with a couple of missing limbs, but the good thing about Shona novels of that time was that like Nigerian movies, getting into the story 25 pages later was no serious setback. The second reason was my late cousin, Innocent (may his soul rest in peace).This naughty fellow had a bookphobia of unimaginable proportions. So he would bring his Shona set books home and during bedtime, instruct me to read for him, a chapter per night. Of course, a couple of paragraphs later, he would be snoring loudly so that anyone who dared to listen from the outside would think that I was performing some incantations to the demonic approval of some dark force.

After sensing an invasion of her turf, Josy later migrated to English novels. However, I suspect that her affair with English novels was not a deep one because instead of citing whole paragraphs like what she used to do with the Shona novels, this time she confined herself to sudden citations of novel titles and their authors. For instance, during a game of bakery (I think that's the spelling; no one bothered to spell the names of games because games were meant to be played), she, from nowhere, announced, *Silent Journey from the East*. So I migrated as well, but unlike Josy, I actually wanted to read the contents of these novels.

Form 1 of course started with the usual: *Mpho's Search*; *Oliver Twist*; *Tunzi, the Faithful Shadow*; *Crossing the Boundary Fence* and so on. Then came Holly Meyers from the United States. She practically upgraded our Rukovo Secondary School library and introduced a reading culture by making sure that every Form 1 pupil had a reading card. In the library, I stumbled upon the Nancy Drew and Hardy Boys series and loved them. I think I read 66 Hardy Boys novels and around 54 Nancy Drews. I usually worked at a rate of two novels per day. Even my English compositions became action-packed, reflecting the influence of America on a young village boy of my calibre.

Then my uncle, Uncle Tich, came to the village from boarding school. Uncle Tich represented what the village was not. He listened to foreign musicians, and usually whistled 'From the Distance' when absent-minded. This song remains a classic for me. There was something foreign and fresh about him that made me want to be his friend. He also brought Dambudzo Marechera (in books and in appearance), Mario Puzo, Robert Ludlum, Wilbur Smith, Jack Higgins, Frederick Forsythe, Eric van Lustbader, Sidney Sheldon, Ken Folliet, Louis L'Amour, James Hadley Chase and many other popular writers.

But the one who really invaded Uncle Tich's life was Marechera. Besides the unlimited collection of expletives that Uncle Tich used when angry or happy, he also began to exhibit behavioural traits that Marechera was famed for. For me, that was what set Uncle Tich apart. It drew me close to him and I became his disciple, reading his books and imitating his English. By the time I reached Form 4, I had read *The House of Hunger*, *Scrapiron Blues* and *Cemetery of Mind* and many other trend-setting Zimbabwean works. I had also read *The Great Gatsby* and many other literary works including *War and Peace*. I was the first, and I am sure the last, to borrow it from the school library. I still remember how I walked up and down the corridors with the book pressed to my chest. *War and Peace* is a voluminous affair and a Form 2 pupil must really be Marecherean to walk around with it.

Uncle Tich had a typewriter. He wrote his stories using that typewriter. I borrowed it from him to type my first story, 'The Mountain'. I deliberately lost it when I came to Harare. Uncle Tich has lost his stories too. He has also lost the Marecherean disposition that made him a rebel of sorts. Now he is all reserved and 'normal' but the linguistic dexterity is still there. A couple of weeks ago, I sent him a poem titled 'Life': "She led me to the house at the end of the street, and left her caresses on my face."[2] He added two lines about "dark voyeurs" peeping at us from the thick but perforated blanket of darkness, and I knew I still had my favourite uncle around.

Now I teach literature at the university. I have all these books in my head, but every time I rattle off some titles like Josy, I am met by blank faces. I don't know if the generation of learners we have now is different from ours, but the truth is that they no longer read these books like we used to. And some of these learners sometimes accost me on campus, or visit my Whatsapp and Facebook inboxes to tell me that they are writing some books. Really?

Hi, I am writing this book…

---

[2] This poem appears in my yet to be published collection, *Because Sadness is Beautiful?*

74

I started studying literature at 'A' Level. I remember that while I was waiting for my Ordinary Level results and herding cattle in the Chiriga hill, I was reading Mungoshi's *Walking Still*. There was a short story that caught my eye. 'The Little Wooden House in the Forest' has a dream-like flow and I decided to writer an experimental short story based on that. A week later, I wrote 'The Mountain', a short story in which a lover who lost his woman to tragic circumstances during a romantic trip to the mountains relives the episode over and over again until he decides to join her. I wrote the short story on some poor newsprint that had blotches here and there from mangoes, soup and *mazhanje*. The story came out well I think.

I wrote another one. This time inspired by Mungoshi's 'The Accident' in *Coming of the Dry Season*. This one was titled, 'The Announcer'. It features a man who was a runner for the 'most patriotic' (you understand why I used these quotes, right?) party in the country, calling people to the party's endless meetings, threatening those who chose to work and not go to the meetings with various forms of frightening things (like flogging at the party office and so on). He is involved in an accident during one of his rounds, and the atmosphere at the accident scene mimics the atmosphere in Mungoshi's 'The Accident'. I later borrowed Uncle Tich's typewriter to type the two stories and hide them in my suitcase for safekeeping.

When the cream and blue-coloured ZUPCO chicken bus (and oh! Did I tell you that I am currently writing *Zupco Diaries*?) arduously transported me to Masvingo, to be transported by Mhunga and Sons Bus Service (it was some kind of relay) to Harare to start my A Level studies, I carried my short stories in my suitcase. Well, to be honest, it wasn't really a suitcase, but then that's a story for another day. I was supposed to carry out my studies at Harare High School in Mbare, but then I was told by some authority there that the number of O-passes I had scored was too modest and therefore I didn't qualify to study there. So by some dint of fortune I found myself at Mt Pleasant High School, studying Literature in English (for the first time in my life), Divinity and Geography.

I remember fishing out my two typewritten short stories to show them to a girl who had taken my fancy. She told me she loved them, but was honest enough to tell me that the same did not apply to how she related with me. It was quite heart-breaking (my first heartbreak I am sure) but I am glad I came out of it unscathed. The same cannot be said about the short stories though. I donated them as tissue paper to some denizens of Magamba Hostels who found it treasonous to use as tissue paper newspapers that had the face of the president emblazoned on them. Back then, the then president was always the headline. Nothing much has changed now.

The point I am trying to make is that I wrote two short stories that were inspired by stuff that I had read. We write because we read. To read is to intellectually invest in the art of writing.

So you have this chap who walks up to me and says, "Look, I am writing this book and I want you to check it out for me." And I am like, "Alright, let's have a look." By the way, this young chap does not know you do not just walk up to people and ask them to read your work. Reading other people's work is a job. I must be paid for my services. But I forgive this chap because he has this light in his eyes that shows that he is really serious. A perfunctory glance however shows that he is poorly mimicking so and so, so I ask him, "Have you read so and so's work?" He looks puzzled. He is probably asking himself why the heck I am asking such an irrelevant question. He says, "No, I haven't." "What about this other so and so?" "No". "What about…?" "No". The No's are so generously pronounced that I decide, remorselessly, to hand back the chap his book.

That's the kind of trouble I run into most of the time. I am now convinced that many writers, especially upcoming, from Zimbabwe, do not read each other's works. They do not read many works from beyond our borders either. Their culture of reading is so dead that what we write is also dead. So we have kids (both physically and metaphorically) thinking that they have written this big thing, but when you get to it you see that it is a poorly done parody of someone else's well-written book which the kid did not read. Sometimes, while reading someone's draft, I feel that if they read so and so's work they can actually improve their own. When I break the news to them, I sense the reluctance to read. The more careless ones take their work and disappear for good, only to surface with a Whatsapp message consisting of a poster that is inviting me to a book launch!

The older generation of writers must be looking at us with trepidation. What can the future hold when it is in the hands of these kids?

Then there is this one who hires editorial services with a launch date and venue already set...

In the Literature Today column of *The Herald* of 11 November 2016, Stanely Mushava wrote passionately concerning the downside (it also has an upside) of self-publishing. In a paragraph that lyrically captured what had been boiling in my heart for a very long time, Stanely wrote: "When one sees a novel, for example, in low-cost packaging, with a cliché, a tasteless bouquet of platitudes and contrived plots, they are bound to miss the good old days when the tradition was more highly esteemed from workflow to reception." I couldn't have said it better! I am a proofreader and editor. Both proofreading and editing demand rigorous, close and careful reading. In fact, both require the writer stay away from his/her script and let the proofreader and editor do their work. Professional proofreaders and editors do not work for free.

They are professionals who have reputations to protect. So when they start working on a script, they want to give it their best.

But they can't give it their best when an impatient writer is nagging them for the script a few days after submitting it for editing and proofreading. Some even give you the launch date to scare you into working fast. But what they are forgetting is that part of editorial work sometimes involves making radical changes to a story, hacking off huge tracts of it and suggesting additions that are almost tantamount to re-writing the story. So how on earth will you do that with a launch date and venue all set? As an editor, I may even suggest that the story is too poor to go out there and needs extensive and rigorous work and research. How are you going to do that with the launch date and venue already fixed?

I am also a literary critic and reviewer. I receive many copies for reviewing. The bulk of the copies I have received this year are products of self-publishing. Some have been successfully read by my wife (Mama JC) and myself. Others have messed up our appetite for reading right from the cover page! So we have left them to gather dust somewhere on the bookshelf. Others have had the misfortune of being in JC's crawling path and he has done a good job of matching their physical appearance with their technical shortcomings. Now there is a second one called Stephanie. Soon she will be crawling. So the danger is real.

Last year, I received a script from a certain fellow who thinks he has been called to write a motivational message for Zimbabwe, especially the Zimbabwe of 'new' dispensations (in poetry I prefer the phrase, 'new dispersion'). I perfunctorily glanced at it and concluded that it needed a generous portion of time and will on my part to exorcise it of obscurity. The chap did not have that amount of time; so he took his script elsewhere only to turn up three days later lugging two cases of books that could fill a modest bookshelf like mine. He was smiling. "Mr Chidora, may I present to you my first book!" I received a copy for "reviewing". Unfortunately, the book found itself in JC's path and . . . you know what he did, lol!

I think an honest reader pointed out the serious shortcomings of the book to the fellow because a few weeks later, after the euphoria of having published his first book had evaporated, he came back to me, repentant-like, and begged me to edit the 'published' book in preparation for the second edition. I told him I needed a soft copy. He promised to send it. That was it. Now I hear the second edition is out although there is nothing "second edition" about it.

It is becoming difficult to find a book in Zimbabwe, written by my generation of writers, which you can read seamlessly without that jarring sensation that is provoked by misplaced words, punctuation errors and misspellings. It's really difficult. It's either our writers are not choosing professional editors or they are not giving the editors enough time. Or it might be because the self-publishing route has made writers escape the rigorous investment of time and money that real editing and proofreading require!

The solution to mediocrity is clear: as a writer you need professional and reputable editors. They will charge a fee and you must be ready to pay. They will take their time and you must wait. They will give you advice and you must heed it. That's the solution. This is part of what it takes to be a writer. It's not just a matter of putting pen to paper. There is more to writing.

If an editor gives you advice and you do not follow it, it's an insult to associate their name with your work. An editor has a reputation to protect because editing is a business. But it's not just the editor who has a reputation to protect; the writer also has a reputation to build. There are two kinds of reputation: good and bad. So as a writer you really need to invest into that process that builds a good reputation for you. The publication of a technically flawed book is, bluntly speaking, a waste of time. Once readers discover that you love wasting their time, you have lost them, sometimes for good.

A story with misplaced punctuation marks, grammatical errors and a serious disrespect for the traffic rules of words does not stand a chance of being read. It takes one bad book to soil a writer's reputation. Sometimes it's not just the reputation of the writer that is soiled but also the reputation of books in general. That's the truth!

In this day and age when the hard-copy reading culture is waning, bad books must not, should not, see the light of day!

Everyone has a story to tell, but how it is told, how it is packaged, is as important as the story itself. My hope is that the self-publishing alternative that our writers, established and new, are embracing is also accompanied by proper publishing processes especially editing and proofreading. I am a proponent of democratic writing space, but I am not a proponent of mediocrity in the name of democratisation.

A word of caution: these accusations of mediocrity exclude Brian Chikwava's *Harare* North or Ken Saro Wiwa's *Sozaboy*. Readers can tell the difference between linguistic deficiency and art. *Harare North* and *Sozaboy* are art through and through. The narrators' bastardisation of English is intentional. But I can't say the same concerning some books that I received for reviewing this year. Maybe one day, after reading every well-written book on my bookshelf, I will turn my attention to these books just to have a good laugh. But for now, let me remain silent!

I have this book I want you to review…

Then there is this other chap who wants me to review their book. They know I run a blog, and a column in the local daily, and so having me review their book is good for business. So they decide to send me a review copy in the form of a PDF that comes on Whatsapp and must be downloaded using my data. The PDF is a poorly done affair: some chapters begin after acres of blank spaces; some words are illogically spaced as if Lucifer has appropriated the spaces between for his insidious tomfooleries. Then I must read the PDF on my phone, or coerce my young brother who has an assignment to work on to give me his laptop (I am the one sending you to school, remember?). The poor fellow has no option.

When I am lucky, I actually receive a hard copy to review. Sometimes it tells me if the future is bright or not. A book whose author has really invested time and money in is easy to tell. I know we are encouraged not to judge a book by its cover, but I usually do that. People do that. There is nothing you can do about it. The best you can do is create a good cover for your book. Then, while I am still evaluating my luck, I receive a Whatsapp message from the author who is enquiring if I have forgotten that the book costs RTGS50. "What?! You mean I was supposed to pay?" I ask, astonished. Then the chap stammers an answer, "Ummm, you see sir, it's like...you know..."

But wait until you hear news of a book being launched in town, and then nothing happening after the launch. The book is nowhere to be found. Not online. Not in the few bookshops in town. Not even on the author's person. The book was launched specifically to disappear. And the publisher... well, that one was set up specifically to publish that particular book! So there is no publisher to contact. And because no one is talking about the book, no one is saying it's good, no one confesses to having read it, you decide to let sleeping dogs lie.

Are you saying this because you studied Literature?

No! But that doesn't mean I should demand that good books be written.

In fact, let me confess how bad studying literature to PhD level is if you are thinking of becoming a writer.

I am widely regarded as a writer in many circles. Even my business card, blog site, Facebook page, Instagram page, Twitter handle and many other pages, state first and foremost, that I am a writer and literary critic. But my CV so far does not contain a single creative writing project. Rather, it contains a list of critical works.

For some time now, I have been plodding along in *Magamba Hostels: a memoir that is not a memoir*. And recently, I started *Zupco Diaries*. These diaries are twofold accounts of a commuter's experiences aboard a ZUPCO bus from February, 2019 to December, 2019, that is, if by December 2019 ZUPCO will still be operational. Things have a tendency of happening too fast in Zimbabwe. On 17 July, I wrote the following diary entry:

When they told me that Vanda was dead, I stared into space, unseeing, seeing only a movie reel of everything that was Vanda flashing before me, to stop abruptly at Vanda standing under the tower light with his friends, painting the air above him with crawling wafts of marijuana smoke, and saying to me, mudhara huyai mumbopuller mbijana ka. And I remember taking generous pulls, pulling and pulling and hearing voices in my head about me being the beloved of blah blah blah, and wondering how the River Jordan could contain the weight of such a revelation. I mean, the sandals, the dove and stuff. It's like you are sitting downstream and the Jordan suddenly decides to give you a dose of reality and you discover in its murderous tempest that being the beloved ain't kids play and all you can do is tuck your tail hurriedly between your legs and raise enough dust for the Jordan to be blinded. Later before going to sleep, Vanda sent me an app message and told me that the grade he had given me was from Malawi or somewhere of that sort. Then the following day, Vanda is gone. I mean, how do you balance that? Can someone please balance me?

The amount of creative exertion that I had to dispense to conjure those few words into life is short of extra-terrestrial. Sometimes, I perform self-diagnosis and conclude that I am suffering from a disease that is fashionable among writers – writer's block. But then I ask myself, *kuti mwana wekuMagaba angazwa zvinhu zvakadai here?*

82

My recent diagnosis has to do with schizophrenia. I think I live in many worlds. I have always lived in multiple worlds ever since the monolithic narrative of my village life was cut short by a Hardy Boys and Nancy Drew invasion, at which point I strove to see Chet Morton in his jalopy (whatever that was) munching a hamburger (whatever that was, again). It was no mean feat, especially when you were herding cattle atop the Chiriga hill to the south of Mutirikwi Dam.

Then fortune provided me with an aunt who whisked me away to the city, for the first time since my born day, to study A-Level. I woke up in Magamba Hostels in the morning to spend the day in Mt Pleasant. It was like crossing the boundary fence. Sometimes I ask myself, should I write about Magamba Hostels or my village? But even recreating my village is no mean feat. Many times I go there, I feel like Lucifer, like I am just passing by. This has been exacerbated by the recent *lantana camara* invasion that has turned the once familiar plains into unfamiliar spaces. So, I go back to Charles Mungoshi's 'If you don't stay angry and bitter for too long' in the hope of gleaning something that can help me write about my village in a more meaningful way.

The thing with being a literary critic and a writer is that the heightened and blatant self-consciousness that you wield as a literary critic keeps interfering with you every time you try to write. When I wrote 'The Mountain' soon after writing my O-Levels, I was an innocent young fellow with little experience of the world of books. Years later, after reading and critiquing many short stories from the likes of Anton Chekhov, Ernest Hemingway, Luis Bernado Honwana, Memory Chirere, NoViolet Bulawayo and others, I feel remorseless about making 'The Mountain' go through the trauma of wiping a patriotic citizen's backside. I do not regret losing the short story.

I am a writer, yes, because I have written some critical works, but right now my obsession with writing creatively has made me think that to be a writer is to be a novelist, a poet or a short story writer. As a critic, I have heard so much about what others say concerning so-and-so's work – the syntax, the themes, the worldview, the intention, etc – and I have even contributed my own share of such critical views by saying so-and-so should have written like this, or so-and-so failed to see that, or so-and-so could have depicted this phenomenon like this.

So, when I attempt to write creatively, I hear all these voices, mine included, laughing in the background at my failure to see this or that.

For example, if there is one character I have struggled with in *Magamba Hostels*, it's the hostel bully. This hostel bully, I tell myself, sometimes vacillates between being NoViolet Bulawayo's Bastard or Richard Wright's Bigger Thomas (before the crime).That's where the struggle comes in. I want a hostel bully who is fresh from the oven, someone never seen before except in my *Magamba Hostels*. I don't know if I am going to pull this off, but I will try.

Then there is this busload of theories that I have been using to critique other people's works: feminism, Afrocentricity, post-coloniality, queer theories, post-modernism, etc. it does not help that I teach Theories of Literature at university. All of them are clamouring for my attention and causing, in the process, a din that continuously saps my creative energies. The recipe of instructions on how to, and how not to, that sits before me destroys my impulsive creativity. The tyrannical voice of theory keeps taking my mind for a walk down corridors of theory when the only thing I want is to write my stories and not give a damn about what so-and-so said.

When the critic is also a writer, which identity, if I may ask, is central? Which one is tucked into the other? The truth is, when people read *Magamba Hostels* (that is, if I finally manage to lay down this critical garbage that is slowing me down), or *Zupco Diaries,* or the collection of poems that I submitted to a publisher recently (*Because Sadness is Beautiful?* is the title), I want them to understand me as a writer and not a critic, and when they read my critical works, I want them to understand me as a critic, because we can only give to criticism what belongs to criticism and to narrative what belongs to narrative.

Now do you see how I am in a quandary too, and that whatever I have said is not being said because I occupy an ivory tower of sorts but because I actually want to see my generation of writers reaching and surpassing the same heights that the older generation of writers reached!

Where to from here

I have often argued that there is nothing new under the sun every time someone came to me with the argument that I should write new things. But I think my argument basically sums a truth we need to accept. Whatever you are going to say, someone might have said it. So if that is the case, how do we circumvent the problem I highlighted earlier, the problem of mimicking poorly what others have written? By reading other writers, discovering how they have expressed what we want to express, and going a step further. Or we can create insaan soup. If you were once a bachelor like me you will probably know how it works. *Matemba, machunks, mazai* and *mufushwa*, all in one massive pot!

I have been told by an eminent writer, that my poetry vacillates between Hove and Marechera. This means it's not Marechera through and through, right? It's not Hove through and through, right? But the truth is these two are some of my best poets from Zimbabwe. So when I write there are things that they did with verse that find themselves in my work. I think that's how we create good literature (well, I am not saying mine is the next big thing). Recently, Rosa Tshuma's Zamani from *House of Stone* has been compared to Rushdie's Saleem Sinai in *Midnight's Children* and Charles Kinbote in Vladimir Nabokov's *Pale Fire*. But I think I can safely say there is evidence in *House of Stone* that Rosa Tshuma is a voracious reader, and that she might have read *Satanic Verses* and *Pale Fire*, but even though that might be the case, *House of Stone* is a stand-alone piece of work. Our works reflect the things/literatures that influence us, and these things/literatures serve to make us better writers. We have more advantages than the writers who wrote before us, because we have more work to read that is at our disposal than them. Lots of work! So the way forward is if my generation of writers become readers, read each other's work, read work from beyond our borders... a practice that will enable them to be aware of how far others have gone and the amount of creative investment that is needed if they are going to be like those writers or even better.

Writers also need to be prepared to invest in the editing of their work. No short cuts. Find reputable editors. At least two. Pay them. Editors do not read books for free. Give them time. Do not come up with the launch date and venue before the final, flawless product is out. Then after these two find a reputable proofreader.

Market your book. As an author, have a plan of how you want your book to get out there. Part of the plan includes review copies. You shouldn't be pestering me to send you Ecocash after giving me a review copy. Make noise about your book. Do everything in your power to make it available. Submit it for national awards even. Try to get it to CDU! Let it be known! Buy other writers' work. Talk about other writers' work on public fora. That way they will buy yours and talk about it.

Conclusion

Zimbabwean Literature, in all languages and genres, started well, on a high note actually. The generation that wrote during "those years of drought and hunger" of the colonial period did a commendable job.[3] We are looking here at the likes of Stanlake Samkange, Charles and David Mungoshi, Patrick Chakaipa, Paul Chidyausiku, Dambudzo Marechera, Musaemura Zimunya, Wilson Katiyo and so on. Successive generations of the likes of Chenjerai Hove, Tsitsi Dangarembga, Shimmer Chinodya, Alexander Kanengoni, Memory Chirere, Ignatius Mabasa, Petina Gappah, Chirikure Chirikure, Brian Chikwava, Virginia Phiri and so on have done a remarkable job. My own generation needs to keep the fire burning. And to do so, we need writers who read, writers who do not do shortcuts, writers who invest time and resources into the work, writers who market their work well. The time to misuse punctuation marks and commit silly grammatical errors is past. The time for clichéd plots is way past. So I am calling on my generation of writers to carry this burden of keeping the literature sector of Zimbabwe alive and healthy.

---

[3] I borrowed this phrase from the title of Musaemura Zimunya's critical volume, *Those Years of Drought and Hunger* (1982).

USED, ABUSED and REFUSED, Part Two
The plight of Zimbabwe's National Liberation War Veterans, 45 years on
Killian Mwanaka (aka Cde Ducas Fambai)

Decent and affordable life

What the national liberation war veterans wanted (in an independent Zimbabwe) was to live, together with the 'povo', a decent and affordable life. A decent and affordable life entailed and still entails having a roof under one's head, owning a piece of land to till crops, having a decent meal (breakfast, lunch and supper) per day, be able to send children to school, access hospitals for treatment and be able to afford other essentials to go by in life. As national liberation war veterans, our expectations were not for one to become a billionaire with Lamborghinis and Ferraris, own thirteen farms or live in a thirty-roomed house.

Coming out of the assembly points and wherever we were, we had nothing in material possession to talk of. We had no home, no clothes and shoes (except what we had on our person), not even a bed to sleep on. Nothing! And, to make matters worse, the majority of us had no meaningful education. Years of formal education had been lost in the war.

We were surprised, as we left the assembly points and interacted with the 'povo' that most of our colleagues who we left behind when we joined the armed struggle, were now living a successful life as doctors, lawyers, engineers, teachers, bank employees, civil servants …; they were living in beautiful houses and driving nice cars. We envied them and patiently waited for our new government to engage us in productive programmes that would change our lives befitting our sacrifice.

In today's Zimbabwe, our plight as national liberation war veterans, is there for everyone to see. One needs to be there – at a national, provincial, district or burial gathering – where we are gathered in large numbers, to witness our suffering. Our sight is pitiful. (Kunzwisa tsitsi kwechokwadi). Here you see us in tattered clothes, torn shoes that show toes protruding and physically, we look a spent force. The mere sight of us is an indicative of poverty. Most of us live in decrepit housing structures while our 'chefs' live in gilded palatial mansions. Our whole picture depicts a dejected and forlorn tribe, abandoned and lost and truly seeking redemption. If one had any modicum of conscience, the question that comes to mind is, "Are these the people who fought for the liberation of our country?" And, befuddled, one leaves shaking his/her head.

Axe to grind

As if he had an axe to grind with the national liberation war veterans, former President Robert Mugabe opted to leave out the very 'comrades' who put him into power in preference for povo, when he appointed his first ministerial cabinet, which ironically had some faces from Ian Smith's government. He made sure that only very few national liberation war veterans were included in his new government. Notable among national liberation war veterans, chosen by Mugabe were, Cde Teurai Ropa Nhongo (Minister of Youth Sport and Recreation), Cde Robson Manyika (Deputy Minister of Labour and Social Welfare), Cde Rex Nhongo (ZNA Army Commander) and Cde Josiah Tungamirai (Zimbabwe Airforce Commander). Edgar Tekere, Enos Nkala, Dr Herbert Ushewekunze and a few others were included into Mugabe's government, but these were not national liberation war veterans per ser. They were typically the arm-chair nationalists who directed war from Maputo, Lusaka and the rear bases. Mugabe went on to choose Provincial Governors and Administrators at the exclusion of national liberation war veterans. From among national liberation war veterans, only Mark Dube (Comrade Joshua Misihairambwi 'Cde Joshuwaras'), was installed as Governor for Matabelelland North.

It is not true to say that among the rank and file of national liberation war veterans from both ZANLA and ZIPRA, there were no suitable candidates to fill some ministerial and provincial posts. We had and have, among us national liberation war veterans, doctors, lawyers, engineers, journalists, business-people... who could easily have handled, with proficiency, some ministerial, provincial and district posts. National liberation war veterans were baffled at seeing opportunistic charlatans like Webster Shamhu given ministerial positions by Mugabe, leaving out the likes of Dzinashe Machingura, Parker Chipowera, Kenneth Taitezvi, Dr Matthew Mudambo (Tendai Pfepferere), Jeremy Brickhill, Flavion Danga, Happison Muchechetere, Dr Mudzingwa, Felix Chemandiwe and a host of other true veterans of the war of liberation. On the women's wing of the national liberation war veterans, we had the likes of comrades Freedom Nyamubaya (late), Irene Zindi, Margaret Dongo, Phideas (sister of Cde Felix Chemandiwe), Karen Nehanda, Tonderayi Mudambo (wife of Dr Matthew Mudambo), Maggie Chikunguru (late), Thandiwe Ngulube, Lorriet Nyemba ... who could have been excellent administrators at national, provincial or district level. But all these were shunned as national administrative positions were awarded to the 'povo'.

Mugabe's strategy of picking only a few national liberation war veterans and giving them positions, in his new government, amounted to 'divide and rule' as this created a schism between privileged and non-privileged national liberation war veterans. And arguably, those (national liberation war veterans) Mugabe picked for inclusion into his new cabinet, cannot be said to have been the most brilliant and brainy among the broad spectrum of the national liberation war veterans.

Moribund and festering with maggots

Astonishingly, as we lived in our limbo of expectation, we realised that our 'chefs' had now ensconced themselves in the plush suburbs of Borrowdale, Highlands and Mt. Pleasant ... while we were homeless and unemployed. And their children were being chuffer-driven to schools. Some of our 'chefs' children were being sent abroad to the UK, Canada and the USA so that when they come back, they would occupy high positions in government.

You needed a special appointment to visit any of the 'chefs' as they swivelled in expensive arm-chairs in their offices. Dressed in pin-stripe suits, they looked at you as if they never knew you and spent the shortest time with you. We were now 'undesirables' to them. In the midst of all this, we realised that some, amongst us, were being hand-picked for jobs or promotion. This was happening in the army, police-force, civil-service and anywhere in the public and private sector. You had to know someone, friend or relative, to do anything meaningful in life. This was the beginning of corruption which, like a cancerous wound, festered and mushroomed unchecked till today. Now the country is like a giant elephant, moribund and festering with maggots.

What became apparent, as life drifted, was that we were living in divergent worlds with our ruling government and party elite. We were living in dreadful poverty while they were living a life characterised by corruption, aggrandisement and profligacy. Our lives, vis-a-vis that of our ruling 'chefs', could aptly be compared to that portrayed by George Orwell in 'Animal Farm'.

Demobilisation money, that most of us received, was a pittance. Consequently, we spent most of it in pubs and beer-halls as we downed our sorrows.

When, under the Zimbabwe Liberation War Veterans Association, led by Dr Chenjerai Hunzvi, the national liberation war veterans were awarded a lump sum of Z$50,000 compensation from President Mugabe's government, the nation faced a monumental financial crisis. Fifty thousand Zimbabwe dollars was a huge amount of money then. However, this money (approximately US$4,500 then) would not buy one a house in Highlands and a Toyota Cressida. At most, it was enough to buy a house in Mbare or a stand in the low-density areas of Harare. The pay-out to so huge a number of national liberation war veterans (in the region of 70,000), drained the national coffers. This raised a national outcry that the national liberation war veterans had arm-twisted the government.

Swimming in untold wealth

When we trained as guerrilla fighters as ZANLA or ZIPRA, in our respective bases, we complied to strict discipline; rules were set and as cadres, we followed those rules without question. We all got in line and conformed. We were a disciplined military force.

We paid total allegiance to our respective parties of ZANU and ZAPU. As ZANLA cadres, orientation taught us that ZANU, and only ZANU, will rule Zimbabwe to eternity. This fanaticism is epitomised (in ZANU-PF circles) in the saying that, 'ZANU-PF ichatonga kusvika madhonngi amera nyanga!' (ZANU-PF shall be in power till donkeys grow horns).

92

For over forty years, since Zimbabwe became independent, our life as national liberation war veterans has been characterised by misery. For the same period, the life of our 'chefs' has been that of opulence and lavishness. The irony of our plight is that we have national liberation war veterans in high places in government of the likes of Oppah Muchinguri (Minister of Défense), Dominic Chinenge (Vice President Chiwenga), and several others in the army and civil service, who went through what most of the national liberation war veterans went through, who know what 'matekenya' are, who were bitten by mosquitoes, but are now detached from the rest of the national liberation war veterans as they 'swim' in untold wealth.

Despite our misery, ZANLA national liberation war veterans have been the staunchest supporters of ZANU-PF. Zimbabwe's national liberation war veterans would die for ZANU-PF and, conversely, would kill for ZANU-PF. We would do this even if ZANU-PF 'chefs' glaringly went astray, like Robert Mugabe did before he was ousted by the current President, Emmerson Dambudzo Mnangagwa. National liberation war veterans are staunch supporters of ZANU-PF and government even if they are kicked in the teeth. The relationship of Zimbabwe's national liberation war veterans and ZANU-PF and government is like that of a master and his dogs. The master is ZANU-PF and government, and the dogs are the national liberation war veterans. The master, together with his dogs, goes out to hunt in the forest. The dogs chase a deer and catch it. When the master arrives at the kill, he slaps the dogs with his back hand and kicks them hard before grabbing the deer away. When he arrives home, the master goes on the table for a sumptuous meal of the deer. He feasts, with his family, and the bones and other undesirable remnants from the deer are the ones he throws to his dogs.

Our blind loyalty, unquestionable allegiance and total fanaticism, have been our undoing as national liberation war veterans. For us national liberation war veterans, ZANU-PF and its leaders are never wrong; they are infallible like the Vatican's Papa. This was epitomised by the fact that we still shouted, "Pamberi naPresident Robert Mugabe!", even moments before he was ousted.

We have been made to live in a ZANU-PF silo where critical thinking is denied. Critical thinking prompts the mind to question in order to get answers. Critical thinking demands the mind to discuss issues and less so, events. Critical thinking desires change (for the better). All revolutions (of the oppressed) were born of critical thinking. Critical thinking refuses the moribund past, static present and constantly seeks change (for the better). Critical thinking demands revolution for transformation and total change. Critical thinking demands action, not rhetoric.

Fanaticism has not helped our cause either. Fanatics hero-worship their leaders. Fanatics view their party's ideology as infallible. Fanatics are praise-singers. Fanatics are parochial-minded. Fanatics are not critically conscious. Fanatics are followers. Worse still, fanatics kill to defend an 'ideology' even if it (ideology) is dead or has long lost meaning. Fanatics are generally ignoramuses. Most of us national liberation war veterans would appear lost if we were asked, 'What is your party's foreign policy?' or 'What is your party's domestic policy?' It is undeniable that, as national liberation war veterans, we have been ardent fanatical followers of the party, to be used as robots or zombies without questioning.

It is highly important to take cognisance of the fact that ZANU-PF and government leaders have plunged the country into the economic quagmire it (country) is immersed in today. It is unfortunate and sad that we (national liberation war veterans), have been used to destroy the country. We are complicity in destroying our country. This is the reason why most of the people of Zimbabwe hate us. Stand in Harare's First Street and shout, "Guys, look here. Look at me. I am a war vet!" They will look at you and almost spit in your face. They will be shot of lynching you.

'ZANU ndeye ropa'

One major problem with us, national liberation war veterans, is that we believe our 'chefs' have our concerns at their heart. No, they don't. Their appetite and ruthlessness to satisfy their insatiable greed for money and power, is there for everyone to see. They wouldn't be living the lavish life they live, feeding their dogs and cats with cakes and milk while we live in shacks and starve if they loved us. But one thing for certain is that they need us. They need us at their convenience. When they want to use us. Come the next election and you'll see them coming to us asking us to campaign for the party. And after we have beaten up and killed members of the opposition parties, chanting, 'ZANU ndeye ropa', and the party wins the election by all means, what do they do with us? Ditch us, the way they have done countless of times before, the way they know best, the way one uses a toilet paper and throws it deep down into the shit-hole of a Blair toilet.

If the Zimbabwean politicians, especially the ruling elite, were asked their honest opinion of us national liberational war veterans, they would, without doubt and hesitation, recommend us to be sent somewhere, away from their sight, where they don't hear us disturbing their peace with welfare and pension demands, heroes' recognition, health-service security and other issues. To them we are the scum of society, a sick entity that needs housing in a sanatorium. If we should appear to them, it is only when they want to use us, especially at election time. Our 'chefs' would be most willing and happy to see us confined in caves as troglodytes.

But, logically-speaking, it is them (our elite chefs) who should serve time in a mental institution because there is no human being, there is no one (on earth) in his/her sound mental faculty, who owns a Rolls Royce, two Ferraris, a Lamborghini, two latest Mercedes Benz cars, the latest MBW, who lives in a gothic thirty-roomed house who stashes billions of dollars in off-shore accounts leaving out the very people (national liberational war veterans) who made all this happen to him/her, languish in appalling misery. Their callousness of heart is beyond human conscience; it is greediness rarely exhibited by the human species.

The land re-possession of year 2000 saw us, national liberation war veterans, thrown into commercial farms owned by settler commercial farmers and successfully drove them out. The resultant outcome of this exercise was to see many top government and party officials grab multiple farms, leaving most of the national liberation war veterans with nothing, not even a square metre of land to call their own. Mugabe himself is known to have grabbed thirteen farms for himself and his family. How greedy!

It is true that the blood of our brothers and sisters, fathers and mothers, was spilled at Nyadzonya, Tembwe, Chimoio, Victory Camp in Zambia …. and watered the mountains, valleys and planes of Zimbabwe. As true as it is that we were killed, it is undeniable and irrefutably true that we also killed. Vatengesi and alleged vatengesi in the war zones, Chifombo (Nhari insurgent repression), Gukurahundi murders in Matabeleland and opposition MDC murders in 2008.

ZANU's history of killing

I mentioned above that we (national liberation war veterans) were killed but, if the truth be told, we, indeed, also killed. We owe Zimbabweans the truth. The truth about the GENESIS of our party's killings. Chifombo Camp on the border of Mozambique and Zambia was the theatre of the first ZANU pogrom. The massacre that took place at this transit camp was of a grand scale.

Chifombo was a transit camp where fighters from Mgagao military training camp passed through on their way to the war zone. Cadres from Zimbabwe also passed through this camp, en-route to Mgagao Military Camp.

I and a group of about 200 finished training mid 1974 and were sent to a transit camp called Kongwa about 80 kilometres from Dodoma, Tanzania's new capital city. Training had sapped our energy, so we were here to recuperate before deployment to the front. After three weeks, Cde Herbert Chitepo, ZANU Supremo in exile and ZANLA COD (Chief Of Defence), Cde Josiah Tongogara, addressed us.

"Your group is the one to liberate Zimbabwe," I remember well Cde Tongogara bawling at us. Cde Tongogara exuded charisma. He had a rough chiselled bearded face. His stature portrayed a typical guerrilla fighter in the mould of Samora Machel and Fidel Castro. But behind this facade was a character, brutal, cunning and cruel. (Will elaborate later). And raising the AK47 he had in the air, he continued, "You are the group that is going to raise ZANU flag in Harare's First Street." We cheered enthusiastically. He rounded up his address by entering into his favourite Chimurenga song, 'Tinofa Tichienda KuZimbabwe'.

Cde Chitepo's address was more on the diplomatic side. He emphasised that since our war was to liberate the people of Zimbabwe, we needed to exercise discipline among the people. With the 'povo', we were like fish and water. We should not drink, rape or behave disorderly in the war zone. His tone was akin to that of a headmaster's, to students who had finished their examinations and were ready to face the world.

We realised that the hour to go to the front had come. At this stuck realisation, some faces showed fear and others portrayed courage, probably false courage because we knew that, at the front, death was a real possibility and not a remote probability as the comrades we interacted with during training, (those who'd come through Mkumbura area), would narrate stories of combat encounters between guerrillas and the Rhodesian forces in which some guerrilla fighters had died.

We got onto the OAU (Organisation of African Unit) Liberation Committee trucks that awaited us. It took two days from Kongwa, Tanzania to Chifombo Camp. Chifombo Camp bustled with activity with comrades of all ages who had come from the war zone. We stayed for a week at Chifombo Camp.

Our group of 200 was divided into groups of fifties. My group, commanded by Comrade Vhu-u, had fifty-four guerrillas and our task was to go and operate in the Nehanda Sector. Nehanda Sector is the area that we know as Mashonaland Central today. This is the area from Mkumbura on the border with Mozambique to Mt. Darwin and Madziwa to Mazowe. Mvurwi, Mtorasnahnga, Centenary and the adjacent areas were all part of Nehanda Sector.

You would ask, 'Why are you saying all this?' I'm writing this because I want Zimbabweans to know what writers and historians have not written about Zimbabwe's armed struggle. You may call what I'm writing, 'the missing link'. These are gaps of Zimbabwe's history that need filling. And it is us national liberation war veterans who must fill these gaps because some of the events happened right in our eyes.

After being issued with the essentials – an AK47, a bandolier with six magazines, a hand grenade, and a 'sagudhu' (back-pack) stuffed with a blanket, a few clothes, one or two dirty pants and socks – the fifty-four of us trudged our way through the Mozambican patchy landscape towards the Zambezi River. Some among us had LMGs (Light Machine Guns) and land-mines. Most importantly, every one of us carried a canteen (soldier's water bottle) 'chigubhu' full of water strapped on his waist. No matter how thirsty one became, you were not allowed to drink from your canteen. Only after instruction would we drink our water. The command to drink water came in the afternoon. This is the time when we were so thirsty, and our bodies needed water the most. Only a lid-full of the container was allowed to be drunk. We would drink another lid-full before sun-set.

Under the blazing Mozambican sun, with the searing heat baking our bodies, we kept marching on.

We did not carry any food rations, which was a surprise to most of us. In the afternoon and before sun-set, Cde Vhu-u, who had travelled this route may timers before, went out with six or seven comrades and disappeared into the forest. When they came back, the comrades would be carrying mealie-meal and a buck or duiker or a wild pig. The animals were shot from the forest which had abundant wild game, and the mealie-meal was obtained from the Mozambican peasants dotted in the country-side. They also brought pots and cooking utensils from the Mozambican peasants.

For four days, we continued with our journey till we reached the mighty Zambezi River. We were ferried across the big river in two boats, the Samora and Machibhombo, cruised by expert

Mozambican peasants. Not far away from the boat I was in, hippos menacingly blew out water from their noses. As we huddled together in apparent fear, the Mozambican peasant rowing the boat said, "Musacha ma'camarada', ishamwari dzanga.' (Don't be afraid comrades, they are my friends). After crossing the Zambezi River, we walked for about a kilometre and came to a small camp manned by three comrades.

On our third day at this camp, late in the afternoon, a group of about thirty comrades arrived. They were from the front. The commander of the group was Thomas Nhari and his deputy, Dakarai Badza.

This was my first time seeing real combatants from the front. Dressed in cowboy jeans and hats, and with AK47 rifles on their hips, they looked impressively commanding.

After we had been quickly assembled, Cde Nhari gave a brief address.

"Macomrades, the war is progressing well at the front," he said tersely. "But we have issues with the High Command in Lusaka. Cde Tongogara and his group have let us down."

Cde Nhari said although combat operations at the front were going on well, there was a problem with helicopters. The helicopters were incurring many fatalities on guerrillas. Cde Nhari said fighters at the front needed missiles to bring down the helicopters. The High Command in Lusaka had been informed many times of this problem, but no positive response had come, Cde Nhari said. Added to the problem of helicopters, Cde Nhari said the High Command was not supplying the fighters with enough medicines to treat the injured. Fighters at the front also needed money to buy cigarettes and other things, but nothing was forth-coming from the High Command.

As we headed to the war zone, Cdes Nhari and his group crossed the Zambezi River, en-route to Chifombo Camp. At Chiofombo, Nhari's group rounded up everyone and made them aware of their intentions. Cdes Lovemore Chikadeya and Peter Ngwenya who disapproved of the rebels' plans were instantly gunned down.

While at Chifombo Camp, Cde Nhari's group abducted Cdes Vitalis Zvinavashe (Fox Gava), William Ndangana (ZANLA Chief of Operations), Charles Dauramanzi (Logistics), Joseph Chimurenga and Josiah Tungamirai and took them across the Zambezi River to Terceira Base near Mkumbura in Mozambique. Meanwhile a stand-off ensued between the rebels and the members of ZANU High Command as the rebels sought to capture the latter and bring them to Chifombo Camp. The stand-point of ZANU leaders, Cdes Chitepo and John Mataure (Political Commissar) was that Cdes Nhari and Badza's grievances should be listened to. However, Cde Tongogara insisted they should never give in to the rebels' demands.

As the negotiations went on, Cdes Nhari, Badza and Siza Molife met Cde Tongogara at a bar in Lusaka. No resolution came out of their meeting.

On 10 December, 1974, Cdes Nhari, Badza and Cuthbert Chimedza and others travelling in two vehicles, attempted to ambush Cde Tongogara at his home in Lusaka. The mission failed after a shoot-out ensued when Zambian police fired at the rebels. Cdes Chemist Ncube and Badza managed to escape but Cdes Nhari, Tichatonga and Molife were captured. This happened after Cde Tongogara's wife and children as well as 19 ZANU officials including three members of the Dare reChimurenga and several members of the High Command, had been captured by the rebels.

After the failure by the Nhari insurgents to abduct Cde Tongogara, they (rebels) went back to Chifombo to regroup. The rebels, thereafter, agreed with the FRELIMO authorities for the latter to intermediate between the two conflicting parties. In an unsuspecting move, the FRELIMO authorities betrayed the rebels to the ZANLA High Command whose unit, led by Cde Robson `Manyika surrounded them (rebels) at Kamwende suburb of Lusaka and captured them.

Once all the rebels, who numbered over two hundred had been captured, a disciplinary committee to try them was set up. This was during the first week of February 1975. The disciplinary committee was comprised of Cdes Chitepo, Kumbirai Kangai and Rugare Gumbo. While Cde Tongogara was for the idea that all the rebels must be punished harshly, Cde Chitepo's suggestion was that they should be stripped of their ranks and sent for safe-keeping in the hands of the FRELIMO authorities. Cde Chitepo's position led Cde Tongogara to believe that Cde Chitepo was siding with the rebels. After Cde Chitepo had gone back to his home in Lusaka, Cde Tongogara remained at Chifombo Camp where he took it upon himself to punish and punish the rebels severely.

In mid-February, at the orders of Cde Tongogara, about two hundred and fifty rebels were lined up and shot, one after the other, with AK47 rifles. Some were forced to dig their own graves.

Cde Tongogara's wrath did not end here. He made sure that all the rebels' sympathizers had 'to go home'. 'To go home' was ZANU's saying of 'to be killed'.

This meant Cdes Chitepo, Mataure and Madekurozva and others, had 'to go home.' All the three and many more were killed. On 18 March, 1975, in Lusaka, Cde Chitepo's VW Beetle was ripped apart by a bomb killing him instantly. Cde Madekurozva was forced to dig his own grave outside Lusaka and brutally murdered by Cde Cleopas Chigowo (ZANU Security Operative) using a pick-axe. Cde Mataure died in similar circumstances.

This is the GENESIS of ZANU's killings. This is the first time ZANU tasted blood. Real blood. Human blood.

My fellow national liberation war veterans, in the spirit of reconciliation we must STOP further killings. The mantra 'ZANU ndeye ropa' is alarmingly violent and murderous in its connotation. The paradigm shift must be, 'ZANU ndeye Peace!' 'ZANU ndeye Love!', 'ZANU ndeye Development!'

It is us national liberation war veterans who should be at the fore-front of transforming ZANU-PF into a progressive party, a likeable party, a party that exudes love to all Zimbabweans, a true party of the people. If we don't transform ZANU-PF, the party risks going down the unfathomable pit of history like Adolf Hitler's Nazi Party, Malawi Congress Party of Kamuzu Banda, National Advance Party of Augusto Pinochet (Chile) and many other parties whose leaders oppressed their people.

ZANU-PF will never be a party of all Zimbabweans if it governs by selective rules. Why is fertilizer, seed and food-aid given only to its supporters, denying members of the opposition? You think this is being clever? No, that's being daft because the people we are denying these essential needs end up hating us and run away from us. Let us tell the party not to HATE but to LOVE. Whoever is sitting at the top of ZANU-PF's diplomatic desk qualifies to be called an 'idiot'.

Is it not apparent that if we give fertilizer, seed and food aid to all needy Zimbabweans, the recipients will call the party 'a good party', 'a loving party' and vote for it. Love has the power to draw people to you and on the contrary, hatred has the power to create enemies who will run away from you. If ZANU-PF extends love to all Zimbabweans, it would be the darling of every Zimbabwean and with the power of love, would win elections with little effort of campaigning.

Chinodya's Queues still mirrors Zim's problems 15 years later: Between the Lines
Beniah Munengwa

ZIMBABWE is currently experiencing queues, be it for fuel, cooking oil, gas and many other commodities.

Fifteen years ago, Weaver Press published the short story anthology, *Writing Still*, which carried a story by Zimbabwean literature legend Shimmer Chinodya titled Queues, which spoke to the reality of the time when "queues" had become part of life in the country.

This has become an enduring theme that speaks to a country battling an economic crisis for which queues for basic commodities are symptomatic.

Queues, a story which was written at the Caine Prize Workshop in Cape Town in 2003 depicts the life of a man that has "...been queuing up all his life" seeking friendship and tolerance but finding himself in "many a wrong queue, only to be told at the crammed garages of my fantasies that I am in the wrong lane, or to be turned away."

I met Chinodya at the recent launch of the book, *Junctions*, and that stirred my interest to revisit Walking Still, which was edited by Irene Staunton.

I re-read Queues in the context of the queues that I am seeing in my everyday life. The read could be depressing as one realises that independence came with a sense of despair and mistrust that pushed Zimbabwe to the brink.

The majority continues to sink in poverty while the powerful get richer and Chinodya observes that the "national cake was getting smaller, but suddenly everyone wanted a piece".

The story succinctly captures how things continue to deteriorate as the persona looks back with nostalgia to a time when his father could send all his three siblings to boarding school on a milkman's pay and how a loaf of bread cost 12 cents and a kilogramme of meat just a dollar. The standards of living are presented as having fallen.

In trying to rescue ourselves from the mess, Chinodya writes, "We borrowed and borrowed until we borrowed until we borrowed the word borrow."

Whilst the political and economic problems of post-independence Zimbabwe are what makes up the greater part of the story, how men and women relate in and outside unions is a gigantic feature of Chinodya's writings.

The extramarital relationship between Rudo and the iconic Clopas Wandai J Tichafa from Chinodya's classic book, Harvest of Thorns, unravels how wretched society has become as Clopas reflects on the degradation of social conditions, especially for the civil servant whose pay is eroded by inflation at the tick of the clock.

What does a man with a wife but without getting love from her do, if not to move on? But if he does, will he ever find peace in living away from his children?

Through their interchange, the deeper yearnings of a man's heart are revealed: "I told her I wanted a good woman to help me do that, that the best thing for a man was a good woman. A good, funny, honest woman. A woman to enjoy, to like, to love, to talk to, to laugh with, to devour, to feast on."

But, a strenuous relationship that takes a toll on one's psychological tank is always an undesirable one.

Society is presented as full of artificialities including theories that are mostly bar talk. "Perhaps the only 'isms we truly knew were chauvinism and sexism." These are what Chinodya picks as the real components of life for, although despised, they are what people practice.

Through Chinodya's iconic 2003 short story, you get to question why we express awe at the occurrence of queues and shortages in this country we call ours in this day and age. Literature through its power of documentation and reflection demonstrates that there's nothing new about any of the problems that we are facing as a nation and that, to hope will be to waste our time. Queues brushes shoulders with other interesting short stories like Memory Chirere's *Maize*, Charles Mungoshi's *The Sins of the Fathers* and many compact others.

This article was originally published in the News Day Issue of, 28, November 2018.

My Silent Grandmother
Tembi Charles

My grandmother was a curious figure: a petite woman who visited occasionally, to spend time with us, of course, but also to sell all the doilies, bedspreads and clothes that she made from discarded factory offcuts. She needed the money to pay for school fees and to feed many grandchildren under her charge. My grandmother was not taken to words – she spent most of her time working. She was an industrious person who never liked too much talk. Open discussion of any topic was not her cup of tea. So that, when faced with unsavoury bits about someone, present or absent, she would sternly tell everyone to keep quiet. She said that words were very powerful; that once out from under the tongue there was no telling what would happen to them, for they took a life of their own. She believed that things should be kept under wraps, not discussed and aired, debated and turned around and round as people are wont to do. She said that, any bad talk about someone, even if it was a lie, would become truth. It was better to pay no attention to bad talk and to never, ever speak about other people. My grandmother said a secret was only a secret if one sat on it and then took it to their grave.

Even though my grandmother was a silent enigma, except for her sighs and grants, I loved her passionately. Her visits to our home in the city, were special. Much more special was the tasty wild fruit she brought from the village. Everything was packed in plastic packets or wrapped in brown paper and secured with colourful strings. Out came *umtshwankela, uxakuxaku*, and more; sweet wild fruit picked by my cousins back at the village. When one looked at those packets of goodies from home, tied up in old plastics and brown paper, which had been used over and over, one would not want to eat whatever came out of there, but oh, it was delicious. The wild fruit, the mealie-cobs, baked bread and scones. I devoured everything. The money she made from selling her wares was given the same treatment. It was housed in a sock, which was twisted several times, put in a plastic bag, twisted again and then put away safely under her breast.

Normally, my grandmother would arrive late in the afternoon. I would get back home from school and be pleasantly surprised to find her there. Of course, those days, most people never had telephones so there was no making of appointments and "booking" people as is done now. People just arrived – relatives never made known that there were coming. There was no letter; no word of mouth. Extended family just materialised at your door to stay for a day or two, a month or even a year. One was never meant to ask what visitors had brought and when they were leaving. Family was family and people stayed, and ate, and drank without paying for anything. It was one's duty to be hospitable and it was done out of love.

The interesting part of my grandmother's visits was the greeting ritual that happened as soon as my father arrived home from his butchery business. My mother would rush into my room which I shared with my grandmother during her visits and announce to my grandmother that my father had arrived. Custom did not allow my grandmother and my father to have eye contact. A son in law and mother in law should never set eyes on each other. It was taboo. Therefore, my grandmother would prepare for the greeting by pulling a shawl over her shoulders and tightening her *doekie*. My father would make his way towards my bedroom, from the living room where he would have had his tea whilst waiting for his dinner. He would position himself just outside our door, close enough to enable his voice to travel to where my grandmother was sitting. The door would be open just a little, and my father would begin:

Linjani salukazi? How are you all?
My grandmother would answer:
Hayi siphilile Gumede. We are all well Gumede.

And so it would go on:
Banjani abanye ekhaya, libatshiye bephila? How are others at home. Did you leave them alive?
Baphilile Gumede, baphilile sibili. They are all well Gumede, all very well. Izulu? The rains?
Ah, komile qha Gumede, yindlala kuphela! Oh it is so so dry, hunger is coming.

Now and again my grandmother would lean over to steal glances at my father, and he would do the same. But they never actually made eye contact – custom did not allow it. Hiding behind doors and stealing glances at each other was the way it was done. It amused me to no end. It was difficult to reconcile that at home I was taught that eye contact with adults was rude, and yet my teachers at the Anglican missionary boarding school insisted that we do so because averting one's eyes meant that you were a shifty, deceitful person. If only they could witness this ritual between my father and my grandmother.

So that is how it was between my father and grandmother. I often wondered if they knew what each other's faces looked like, if for all these years they never really looked, really looked at each other. Years went by and my grandmother kept coming and going and I continued to witness their strange encounter. I would never have thought that a time would come when our two families would stop being close as a tongue is to saliva, that we would be divided by my mother's death and that my lovely, sweet, headworker of a grandmother would be called a witch. I would never have thought that my father, who had loved my grandmother so dearly would stand so far away from her and declare to all that she was a witch who had killed my mother!

The Poet's Revenge To No One Who Buys Poetry Books
Tendai R Mwanaka

The humans think they have just deleted you, dear poet. No one reads poetry anymore. I mean no one buys our poetry nonsense. Ask them to buy a copy and hear them running hard to find excuses, *"sorry I have financial commitments at home"*, *"sorry I have a school grant to pay back"*, *"sorry the government didn't increase my salary"*, *"sorry my child has just died and I am burying her now"* (the last I checked he didn't have a child, and that's just last month ago!), *"sorry poetry vexes me"* (of course, you are pretty!). And the clever ones will lie to you they will buy a copy every end of every month until you are tired chasing them. I have done these chases and later realized even chasing a Zimbabwean girl for her heart's warm breath is child's play as compared to chasing this lot for their little scraps. You realize, later, they were just being polite, but no, they are not going to buy your poetry nonsense. There poet, you see where your revenge lies. No, they have enough money to buy poetry, where are they getting data bundles to stay online 24hrs a day, seven days a week, and 500days per year. Shut up you I-know-everything, I know your year has 365 days! This book only costs 15 bucks, not 365 days. The truth though resides in these lamessss excuses!

Start with the said government. Revenge for all those years you have tried to be a poet and pay tax and that government you pay taxes to doesn't do a single thing to help you to live like a poet. Mmm I wanted to say *like an artist*…and I was scared my big brother David Mungoshi will kick my butt for using the title of his collection of poetry! After all it's this same government to blame for not increasing the above reader's salary, yet you have been paying your taxes to the same government. That government has grants for farmers, for musicians, for industry, for social services, but not for the poet.

Don't sell your books, Poet. Stop doing books.

Instead mock that minister, mock that president, mock that governor, mock that councilor, the self-important senator. You are safe. That lot stopped reading poetry during Shakespeare's time, so don't even worry about using hidden poetic language. Use the ffff, the ssss words, strip them naked with your sassing words. No one is reading poetry remember so no one will be pissed by your use of these words. No rules apply on you.

Tell that professor fossil at your local university to shut the ffff up about poetry rules. You don't need that poetry education, who the fuck taught Shakespeare? After all, no one is buying poetry so what rules, to do what with them. Write like you have just awoken from the coma you entered before humans were even created and write so far into the future. I am serious, every poet knows the future, to millions and millions of years ahead of his time. Check the bible. Check the bhavagad-gita. Check the koran. Check the African bushman cave paintings. Who do you think wrote those books you are still using several mellenials later and take as the truth? How did the writer who wrote them come to know about you? Show me any other writing that has survived millennials that isn't poetry. Robert Duncan was right (I didn't say correct) in saying poetry resides in the office of God.

Reject everything (when I grow up, I will address this concept).

Ffffff with their grammar rules, ffff their metaphors, ffff similes, ffff images, ffff conventions, ffff alliteration, ffff whatever nonsense they harp about in those lit dead classrooms, making a career over dead poets whom they didn't support when they were alive. For goodness sake Dambudzo slept on park benches in Harare but see the scholarship the maggots have built around him. Where were they when he was struggling? They get thousands of dollars grants to study new African poetry, do they? No, they just copy what you the poet wrote poetically and put it into big, long winded, complex words, then garnish it by quoting one or two other fossil fuel scholar

112

and there; see their bank accounts are honeyed as they go to sleep in the comfy of their leafy upscale homes in borrowdale, upper east, hamptons, sandton, south london, menlyn, ascot and you are left to rot in meru (I don't even know where that is), okay Chitungwiza, Soweto...

Or if one of those braveless little souls so called scholars really focuses on new African poetry and avoids New York Times indicted (I meant dictated but my mind failed to detect the word), African poetry, they will create solid and real scholarship on Africa but that will be the end of study of anything new in African poetry and those lazysss fossil scholars will copy that research for another 50 years until another brave braveless soul decides otherwise. You wonder why the Western Reader is still speaking orgasmically of Brutus, Achebe, Ngugi's Africa, etc… as if we are in the ffffcking 60s, or the watered down version of these you would find in the NYT Africa and The Guardian Newspaper whatnots. To think that less than 2 million American readers and one editor decides for a continent of over 1 billion people what Africa is, safely ensconced in their Western homes and offices. Dear poet, so when that professor fossil fuel start messing you about rules on your fb poetry posts tell him to shut the ffff up or go back to the classroom and boring grant writing. He has no hold over you. Zuckerberg has no University of Facebook, yet!

Write about that next door friend's wife you have been banging behind his back. Tell him in your poetry he doesn't read that you used your poetry to entice his wife into your arms. Don't worry, he doesn't read your poetry, and I bet the whole Mubvumira street's people don't read poetry, so they will never know about this. Write about that thief, the arsonist, that sodomising teacher, but don't go with this evident writing to the law man. You have no duty to a country that doesn't support its poets!

When they expect you to write socially or politically conscious poetry to quote in their politricking as if they are paying license fees for quoting you. Seriously if they were paying, the poet would be a rich middle class dude. Write about the trees, rivers, forests, mmm of high thighed trees, long rivered rivers, dark lingering banks, talk of dams that drips sweet scented enchanted waters, talk of the highs and lows of the rivers' waves, talk of the gorges, the forward thrusts of the river's waters, the sands oozing from your river. At least this oral exercise is beneficial to your broke sss psyche and body.

And when at your church they ask you to write a poem for the church, write it dear poet. No one reads poetry. No one buys poetry books. But know that they had never intended to pay you for that. That they would tell you that you are doing God's work. Ask yourself why they pay their parish priest, the pastors (here we are talking of those millionaire ssssholes) but they expect the poet to work for free because no one buys poetry books. Okay no one buys poetry books for real, that's why I wrote this diatribe. Write about DOG, write dog stuff, write about the dog's thread, write about chickens, about cats, write about sitting on the lawns, drinking cappuccino, swimming, cooking spinach, write about that middle class self-doubt boredom bullshit you find in White Western poetry these days. Write like everything is demanding an apology from you, as if you are responsible for killing everything that died since "In the beginning..." For sure the white man is guilty! And the black man is his hanging god now...

By all means go to the church and read your poem. They don't pay for poetry remember so who do you think you are trying to impress by writing serious stuff here. Not God. He knows everything already.

They say poetry vexes us but they still love and buy music, without worrying about the poetry in the songs. They say everyone is a poet, just like they say everyone is a singer, and if 7something billions of people are poets why the hell is the poet poor and the musician super rich. And if music is poetry on fire as they sometimes say why the hell is the poet excluded from the riches. He is the one who started the fire. So dear poet, do the Little Wayne on them next time they ask you to write them a poem they want to convert to music. *"Mememeeee me, me bitch, kikikiii, uwii humhum, nigger ha, ha dadada, di, ndindi sucker, fefefe, fefeku mullah baby ffff me, phew, grrrr, rrrr, motherfffffer fffff, ssss, aaa, ffff you, Mememeee, me, me, I got money bitch, pfeeeee...."* (I am sorry to the ZANU-PF's Pfeeerorists) I meant mumble, bumble, hark, gag, glut, groan, swore, shiver, puff, spit, whistle, laugh…, haloing rhythmically, like god ffffing Little When, like a bumble bee. Little When is the poet's answer to those ffffers who pay the musician but not the poet.

Why is everyone making money out of you but do not want to pay. Did you really expect me to know the answer?

Ask Zuckerberg. Paperbag created this facebook everyone is spending all their money on, so use this free book of the face to suckerpunch them with your poetry nonsense. They want to read a poem for free, and they will compliment you by liking your love nonsense poetry. Oh, how they like to read this love shit on facebook, and they tell you big black lies about your genius, *"wow"*, *"you are brilliant"*, *"OMG"*, *"you the best poet to ever come from Africa"*(going where), *"oh I have never read anything like that before"*. Yes, of course they have never read anything like that before. They stopped reading poetry books during Shakespeare's time and Suckerberg is only 32. If you think I am lying they stopped reading poetry books during Shakespeare's time, go and listen to Benedette Meyer on audio, in the late 70s speaking to Susan Howe, about Suck Town that will become Zuckerberg Town. She was complaining about readership and support from the establishment poets were not getting (anymore) in Uncle Trump's Towers. How about 50 years later in godforsaken dark Africa?

So instead of serving them the easy to read sweet love or inspirational diatribe they need to make themselves feel good with their nobodyness, rather write number poetry. Do Nicanor Parra on them, write anti-poetry and fuck with that Swedish kangaroo court that tells the whole world who is the best writer. They also do the no-Nobel on you, poet! Where is Nicanor's Nobel speech? If they could give it to the poetry in Bob ffffing Dylan groans, hoarse-shit voice moans, you wonder where is the Nobel speech for

....
....
....
....
....,

go ahead and fill up that space I left with our every year's near miss. As long as they are still alive, please don't provoke those that are with the maker. May God find mercy for their saddened hearts the Nobel Mafia burdened them with? You wonder how they came to read everything that's being written in over 10 000 languages and come to say this is the best writer in the world. It's like those other little sisies competitions like World Footballer of the year (Sorry to the Ronaldites rodents and Messites termites, it's you who crapped on that competition), Miss World beauty competition, Mr Universe (I wonder when they are going to give this to the trees…mmm aren't trees parts of this universe? And they are better people too!). Ffff Nobel, Fffff Guardian Fiction Prize, Fffff Caine Prize, Fffff Pulitzer prize, Fffff DAAD, ffff that dash dash Chapman prize (Chimpanzee), ffff every Literary gangster prize out there. They are not for the poet! I said do number poetry,

1, took 2, to turn 3, to
Ten, twenty metres to
4, took 5 to fight 6, eat
Thirty, pretty, eight, seven

Shiii, shut up professor fossil fuel. This is poetry for the lazy suckers who uses social network to read poetry they don't pay for. They still expect you to dish them a treat every day which they will use to court each other with, make babies on, and build their relationships on. Where is your payment, dear poet? Write that number poetry stuff and help promote population control. They have forgotten for them to be here its poetry that their fathers used to tame that wild Eve that their mum was. They forget that without poetry man is nothing, can't do a thing, and can't even tame the little wench. Go subvocative poet. I did that last year in Logbook Written by a Drifter,

Sub Vocative:
For Norman

Ooe uoi ooo oei eoea
Eoo uii iee ooe eeeio
Aae uioo oeei uiiioeo
Eeoo oiuea aeeiou eui
Aeeeo iouoi eoiuo aeeio

Eouioa
Eiii
Eoiuu
Aooiu
Eiii
Eouioa

Of course they are not going to pay you, so here is the last revenge for you dear poet. Don't stop writing poetry, just to spite them keep writing that nonsense. Write the poetry you want to write. Writing is for you, you need it. Don't worry your time will come soon into the future. The robots are coming to sit on their accountancy, engineering, clerical, fatssss managerial jobs and the safest career is of the creative, so stick to that now, dear poet. You are crazy if you think a robot will ever be capable of creating this diatribe.

But you want to live reasonably well like all these fffers now. So take time to do other things, learn other trades. I advise you to be a farmer. This is where you will ffff them better. Grow food for them and price it high. Its only food they won't find an excuse for not spending those facebook bundles for now. Let them do their facebook shit whilst you are busy watering your carrots, veggies, cereals (I am not talking of Cereal Ramapostponer). Its food here, and then price your foods double the usual price to compensate for your poetry they have been reading for free. You make them woo each other with your poetry so that they will create more humans, whom you will grow food for. Now, you can control them. You have the inside track to both food for the soul and food for the body. This is your Custer's last stand dear poet!

An Interview with Philani A. Nyoni
Jabulani Mzinyathi

Zimbolicious welcomes you to this interview. You are an accomplished writer/poet. That is no secret. The essence of this interview is to inspire upcoming poets/writers in general.

JM: Tell us a bit about yourself, areas of interest other than writing. Hopes, dreams, fears if any

PAN: I'm afraid I'll say too much and kill the mystique. Half my readers want to murder me in distinctly elaborate ways; I can't afford to have them think I'm a half-decent human being who scrubs his teeth twice a week.

JM: To what extent is your writing influenced by your background, if at all it is

PAN: I finished school in a dark period in Zimbabwe. We didn't have internet back then, I had no reasonable prospect of attaining tertiary education so all I had were books, mostly the old English masters so for a long time I laughed at free verse. I still think its liberalism is the wobbly backbone supporting most of naked strings of ideas barely coherent to the sensibility masquerading as poetry. That only half defines my literary conscience.

I've wanted to write since I was ten, I'm told I was rhyming before crèche; I suppose that propensity to musicality makes it easy for me to put out 'loud sounding nothings' in the words of Mattenich on the Versailles Treaty. When I write from within I put out half-decent things. And looking back there are crossroads in my life that stand out as defining points in my career; like the time between the ages of eight and ten when I couldn't speak much. Or when I was fifteen and Emmanuel Mpofu, my history teacher, discovered the Master Copy for all the literary pornography I was feeding pubescent peers and invited me to a treaty-conference which ended with me conceding that my works were more noxious than I had previously assumed. And thus began my tutelage in Walter Rodney, Ngugi et al. That's when I started understanding the traditional role of the African Writer. As I grew in wisdom and stature I began to see the world, I saw hopelessness and somehow refused to let it swallow me. If I can transmute the pain to poetry, or any other form of literature or art, then it would have been worth something.

JM: What genre do you like the most? Why are you particularly drawn towards it?
PAN: I love poetry because I appreciate how hard it is to write; I'd rather argue with fourteen lines than forty thousand words. Strangely I picked up the genre later, well after I had started dabbling. I have though been straddling genres recently, as if my spoken-word isn't dramatic enough I've embarked on a quest to turn poetry into film and stage plays. It worked with 'Jane The Ghost', 'Diary of Madness' and the most daring recent wild-child 'The Passions of Black Jesus' which has only staged at the Harare International Theatre Festival and is yet undergoing heavy modifications.

JM: You are a poet. What type of poetry do you write? Why do you choose that style or those styles?

PAN: I write all sorts of poetry. The best description for it is 'experimental'. My sonnets are loosely confined to the tradition: I love half-rhymes, internal rhymes, sometimes I sonnet with anagrams and it makes me feel good inside. Sometimes I am pissed off and just want to rant, so I write whatever I feel. And I wish I could stop feeling things to write in the middle of the night; but then my deepest joy would vanish.

JM: Which poets or writers have influenced your writing in general? Why are you drawn towards those writers?

PAN: There have been a few over the years, and I think every period has its hero. I learn something from every poet I encounter, because Picasso said great artists steal and I believe him because he was a great artist. Not least because he stole!

JM: Tell us about your published works
PAN: My first title was 'Once A Lover Always A Fool', that was published in 2012. Two years later John Eppel and I did 'Hewn From Rock', I followed it up with 'Mars His Sword' in April 2016, that one holds a World Record, a Special Mention (whatever the fuck that is) from the National Arts Merit Awards and a Bulawayo Arts Award for Outstanding Literary Work. I was done with writing then, publishing at least; until Robert Mugabe was deposed and I felt I had to return to active duty. I put out 'Philtrum' one week after his 'resignation' (if you enjoy euphemisms) and updated it after the current president's inauguration. I'm still to be impressed by any other book on the subject, but then I'm biased. By the time this interview is in print I might have a new one in Sweden.

JM: Are you into self-publishing? What are the advantages and disadvantages if any?
PAN: Yes I am. Ironically it's because of my appreciation of traditional publishing. But it's a tonne of work, I only do it because I started writing at a time when Amabooks was the only publisher of poetry worth mentioning in the country. If I hadn't done that then no one would have put out my works. The state of the industry necessitates self-publishing, but one has to be very wary and conscious of what a publisher really does in order to duplicate the process efficiently. And maybe one-up the traditional publisher. I'm pleased to have developed my skills in the craft such that I moonlight for some publishers in things like typesetting, proofreading and editing. But it isn't a walk in the park. If an entire team can take up to nine months to work on a manuscript after the author has decided

it's done, why would that same author shortchange us with putting it out two weeks after writing the last word? I for one consistently write just about every day, yet have at least two years between publications. I want to be sure. That's the biggest danger with self-publishing: quality control. I have worked with amazing local and international publishers enough to appreciate them. It's not just about copy editing, writers fall in love with lines, some of them are impotent or unnecessary, some are just overly dressed loud-sounding nothings. Writing is emotional, it's like parenting: nobody wants to be told their child is ugly and needs a plastic surgeon; yet too often necessary.

JM: Upcoming writers/poets usually have this perception that there is a clique of writers that have made it that shut them out. What is your take on that thinking?
PAN: It's absolutely true. There is a clique of people who have mutual respect for each other because they have seen war and understand the necessities of getting the job done. They admire each other for what they have endured, sometimes together, to gain their stature and arrange those woods/words so painstakingly. They meet often in the same spaces and ask things of each other that the asked is scared to say no to because of what Paulo Coelho calls 'the favour bank'. The bank and the mutual admiration bordering on fetishism is what makes it easier for them to do things for each other. It's nothing personal, but that's what makes it hard for someone who does not speak the language to gain any traction with this illuminati. When we all come into the industry we all have illusions. Sometimes these writers who seem to have made it share a common disillusionment, sometimes they share a common illusion.

I found the perfect metaphor for life in this journey while hiking in the mountains of Mozambique with a good friend Jenna recently: When you're at the bottom it looks like the top is fifty metres up; then you climb higher and at a hundred and twenty metres you find some people who were so ahead of you, you think the mist on the top is their cooking-fire. So you stand there with them, some are fed up with the climb and will make camp there, some want to go back down already, some are already climbing and won't listen to you, but most of you just hang around together, looking up, discussing which is the best side to scale it from.

JM: How many books have you published to date?
PAN: Three and a half. The half was with John Eppel. All my solo works had been award-winning until 'Philtrum' and its explosive subject-matter. That might seem disappointing until it gets into the hands of a Swedish publisher who decides to put out a new collection of translated works for the Swedish market. So that will be five by the end of the year; I will probably spend a while trying to pronounce the title of my fifth.

JM: Which one is your favourite? Why is that so?
PAN: No parent should ever be made to choose which of his children he loves best; but at gunpoint I would say 'Once A Lover Always A Fool'. Your first project is the longest and most meticulous one. In my most private moments, I concede that I'll never write something as complete. Maybe I have, but I like to think that.

JM: Have you won awards if so tell us which ones?
PAN: A few. I'm the first and only Zimbabwean poet to be awarded National Arts Merit Awards for Literature and Spoken Word. I received my first one for 'Once A Lover Always A Fool' at twenty-three, three years later I earned the Spoken Word one. That's also the same year 'Jane The Ghost', a film I co-wrote and shot won 'Outstanding Short-film'. 'Mars His Sword' received a Bulawayo Arts Award in 2017, the same year it got 'special mention' at the National Arts Merit Awards. My short story 'Celestial Incest' was shortlisted for the African Writers' Award in 2018. Before all that I

received a First Class nod at the Girls' College Literary in 2016 'Honours', the following year along with the 'Best Poem' award for a piece titled 'Shakespeare'. 'Mars His Sword' also set the World Record for 'Most Shakespearean Sonnets in a Manuscript'. It was officially verified by Record Setter and still stands. I wrote 308 at 26, Shakespeare died at twice that age, his official collection has half of that.

JM: Are your works raking in a lot of financial rewards?
PAN: So the taxman sent you this time? Et tu Brute? Next question.

JM: What inspires you to write poetry/ prose?
PAN: The shortest answer is 'anything'. The nature of inspiration has been debated for years, but I like the German attitude towards it: it's possession, the demon is very rude and knocks at strange moments.

JM: What do you think of the state of writing in Zimbabwe currently?
PAN: This is an entire dissertation on its own.

JM: This country is reeling under an economic tsunami, to what extent has this influenced your writing?
PAN: In 2014 Noviolet Bulawayo recommended me to The Caine Prize for African Writing and I spent two weeks crafting a story with some of the hardest fiction writers of my time. Most of them were out there, published by real publishers, international, well-traveled and with fierce reputations. I was just that strange kid from Zimbabwe. My hair was wild, I wore this tracksuit and white t-shirt that should have been relegated to a skorobho a long time ago. I was the youngest among them and probably the least known. I remember how blown away they were the first time I read my project. I also remember how they drove me to drink spirits (I had been on beer

the whole time) the second time they heard me read. One would ask if I wasn't propping up the stereotype of 'poverty-porn' by undressing the regime, I was cautioned by someone who used a pseudonym because they were very-very close to the First Family: they didn't have illusions about what those in power do to people like me. I had been counselled not to 'sell the country' before I went to that workshop but I did. I thought about my situation, what I would go back to when the four-star luxury of those two weeks was over. I lived in a tiny room, slept on the floor, hardly ate for two days within a week of leaving that workshop; I assure you, I had no regrets for writing what I had left on those pages now published as 'The Soneeteer'. I remember my response to the sell-out question, right in front of a crackling fire, drink in hand and barman ever poised to serve whatever poison the spirit hungered: 'if you had one chance to tell a story, and you knew it was going to be published anyway, in ten countries; wouldn't you tell the most important story you had inside you?' The story was that some will never be great or appreciated for their gifts and energy as much as they should be because we are here, now. But while I have this opportunity, I'll punch as hard as I can. Memory Chirere called it 'the craziest story in the book' when he reviewed the collection; it was only a portrait of the times.

JM: There are lots of upcoming poets/writers out there. What advice would you give them so that they really hit some measure of success? PAN: Just write. Read. And write. And read.

JM: Briefly tell us what writing endeavours you are currently engaged in
PAN: I'm always threatening to retire. I had succeeded until the November coup. Right now I feel like John Wick: all I wanted to do was kill the guy who murdered my dog, now I'm tearing through a bunch of bad guys with half the stamina that made my name. I hope

'The Passions of Black Jesus will be my last effort, if not then look out for something called 'Virgin Blood & Lingerie'.

JM: Please, please, please share with us three, of any of your poems

Poems by Philani A Nyoni:

How I Became Spartacus

The crosshairs of fate saw me stark in the street
Amidst a flurry of anger and violence.
I stopped to watch the inferno that had been lit
On the corner of Tenth and Fort, after I'd wept;
Not for the pain in my soul nor the rags
My home has become: brothers devolved to beast
Straining the constrain of a shit-stained flag,
Not for my dreams (not iron) that had been creased
And tossed into the bin alongside my savings,
Their pensions -there is none for what I do-
But the indiscriminate force of police and teargas.
I hid in the library when I was done braving
The assault, walked home ere the sky changed hue.
I should have slept in the next day but the crass
Air called me outside to inhale a country burning.
You should know, as I type this, I'm waiting
For the police to kick down my door and set fire
To my nuts with some electric contraption of torture.
In all this what is my crime? I too wish, nay, aspire
For a new country to be born, but this is my occupation,
I have no employer to raise hell against... or expectation,
And I'm too famous to do crazy shit on the street.
I waved at but did not take part in the demonstration,

126

What I do is more personal, and more discreet.
So you can imagine my consternation, dear reader,
When I found my name in the pages of The Guardian*.
They were right, I think we have suffered enough,
I think the policies of the government are stupid,
But I think the price hike is justified, the dildo currency
Is broken and not trading well beyond our borders.
But I try to keep my opinion of the currency or the men
At the helm out of the media, just in poems and stuff.
But the government has blocked the communication grid
So I can't denounce the devil with the urgency
It demands. So now, I only await the soldiers orders,
Wondering, if the journalists in white countries are like ours
Who make up quotes to spice up their letters.
Surely there are enough corpses to speak the horror.
Maybe some silly fuck protest-brave but shy for the camera
Gave a statement and wrapped it in my name.
Today I have a dangerous name, like Spartacus.
Now I'm not sure if I still want to be famous
(Hearing this my Christian tattoos choired:
To whom much is given much shall be required)
It could also be an elaborate plan to get me killed.
I have a great dilemma my friend, but all the same,
Fuck it, let them come and bury the knife to the hilt,
They can hang me for treason, right next to Corday,
Or put a bullet in my msundulo and... I don't know, say
I evaded arrest and tried to run away from the police gang.
Isn't that what we all want? To go out with a bang?

*We have suffered enough,' said Philani Nyoni, an author who was part of the
protest in Bulawayo. The government is now aware that we are not happy with
their stupid policies like the fuel price increase.' -The Guardian, 14 January
2019

Chimanimani

Some come here to live in tents;
Not these, caught between god and man.
The high wrath that sawed, mountains rent,
Washed them here, to pray in vain
To the kindness of meddlers not long in office
But answered by kindred, slightly less hopeless
While elected seats fly sofas in choppers
Over homes, wives, goats and children
Drowning, floating, to the Indian Ocean.
And the sofas have flown away,
Will they return? Who can say?
When the wives, the children and goats
Decide to float back home?
And now there are only tents to stay,
Not like the tourists', these might be here
Until the rain returns. And beyond.

Nadir

Sometimes I shout so you can hear me.
Between our silences there's a crackling;
My soul in the petals of my yoke; can't you hear?
Not while you're trembling in your pain.
We said love would conquer fear.
Now our love is aching.
I reach for your face, it's all in vain,
Night and timezones won't let us be;

So I scream because you are far
And winter's rattling on my scars
And I should remind you to die only once;
To carry those who go before you,
Don't follow them into the ground.
But you can't hear me like it's not aloud
And I'm scared of what I'm about to do:
Cut you deep so you spare me a glance
If my worth hasn't faded after our dance,
Wasn't just a boy you needed to feel young:
A drought of skunk to shake your lung.
I'm screaming! hoping you hear me
As if your sadness could ever cheer me.

"The Word is gibberish, the plot Absurd."

-Derek Walcott

JM: Lastly Zimbolicous thanks you for taking time to participate in this interview. All the best in all you do.

From Colonial Master to Enemy: Issues Behind Zimbabwe-Britain Relations in Post-Humanistic Histories.

Zvikomborero Kapuya

Abstract

The study examines the British-Zimbabwe relations in the 21st century and adopts a rigorous intellectual analysis of some of the unchartered terrains of knowledge. It is argued that, coloniality of land, power and global space is the main driver of the hostility since Zimbabwe's protracted land struggle from 1893-2002 threatened Pax Britannica and Western hegemony, resulted to sanctions. In current media reportage and literature, it is argued that, Zimbabwe was sanctioned as a result of non-compliance to the dictates of democracy and property rights through orchestrated violent land invasion without compensations, but history repeats itself, what happened in 1893-1896 also happened in 21st century were land was given back to the original owners. The research use desktop reviews and employ Transmodenity, post-structural, realism and post-modern theories to cement arguments.

Key Words: Land, Coloniality, Decoloniality, Zimbabwe, Britain
Introduction

International system is characterized by the discourse of change and continuity, that parade as the dynamics of international relations. The central issue of this article is the factors that led to the deterioration of the relations between Zimbabwe and the West, there are number of factors that establish an epistemic hypothesis over this phenomenon. The relations between Zimbabwe and the West date back in pre-colonial, colonial and post-colonial episodes, in this question the main focus is 'post-colonial Zimbabwe". To comprehend this discourse, the philosophical thoughts of Zimbabwe-West relations informed by theories of the international relations that simply explain the behaviors of the state in global affairs. Fukuyama (1991) coin the theory of 'end of history' whereby the liberal-capitalist triumph over socialism, but 21st century political affairs proves Francis Fukuyama theory wrong, the centrality of the discourse of relations and conflicts in Zimbabwe-West relations remain a key evidence to object the claim of 'end of history'. It can be said, 'history truly was ended but returned from vacation in the post-millennium society'. There are various factors that deteriorate relations of Zimbabwe-West, manifest in form of political, social and economic, however basing on this means of analysis, termed the trinity of analysis by Wallenstein (1991), argues that it limits the analytical concept of the discourse hence this article is focusing much on developing the epistemology of foreign policy analytics and the issues that led to the sour relations of Zimbabwe and the West. Political factors are more important in this discourse, since politics define the global interaction, issues of anti-imperial legacy, land redistribution, democratic crisis and abuse of human rights (property rights), however there are some other factors to look on for instance, social factors such as racism and economic factors as to proffer a clear proposition of the central problem. Events such as land reform programme, sanctioning of Zimbabwe, electoral violence and the Look East Policy are key concepts in elucidating the factors that contributed to the deterioration of Zimbabwe-West relations. To engage in critical taxonomy of this aspect, realism theory, game theory, idealism theory, dependency theory and Marxist theories provides a theoretical paradigm to comprehend the contemporaneous issues of Zimbabwe international relations.

Intellectual Analysis of the Issues Behind: Confrontation or Justice?

To commence, the issue of land reform policy remains a central issue in the understanding of the deterioration of Zimbabwe-West relations.

The available literature engages in researches from different disciplines with different narratives that are informed by Chimurenga culture and non-partisan perspectives (Mahomva 2016). The idea of decolonization was an unfinished project in 1980, whereby means of production controlled by few white minorities protected by colonial Westminster legal statutes, the Lancaster House Constitution, Chapter two on Human rights. Against this background, land was the central issues of conflict during the war of liberation struggle (Muchemwa 2013, Mutizira 2008 and Nyawo 2012). This simply explains that, land was the strategic factor for Zimbabwe diplomatic relations with the West, hence Mugabe regime embarked on land reform programme as to achieve the objectives of War of Liberation Struggle and decolonization.

"For a colonized people the most essential value, because it is the most concrete, is first and foremost the land: the land which will bring them bread and, above all, dignity" (Frantz Fanon 1963).

In Fanonian school of thought, the marginalization of blacks (dames) to reserves matured into conflict, that kick started the project of liberation, later continued in the post-colonial Zimbabwe. As to establish a post-colonial society, Mugabe's regime embarked on Land Reform policy, sloganized the motto of correcting imbalances and termed it "Hondo yeminda" (war of land). This event created a most decisive effect to the almost tattered Zimbabwe-West relations, and violated the Lancaster House Conference Agreement of the land question and white settler. In analysis, the Fanonian school of thought provides an epistemic paradigm about the value of land, whereby it gives dignity to the people and above all as source of economic production, against this aspect the political reclamation of land by the native Zimbabweans who were once marginalized in the colonial era, aimed to restore the dignity and pride, affected Zimbabwe's foreign affairs. The land question contributed immensely to the deterioration of Zimbabwe-West relations.

Furthermore, the aspect of anti-neocolonial campaign manifest in the philosophy of Mugabeism had much effect in further tearing apart the relationship between Zimbabwe and the West. Scholars and diplomats, largely concern about the logic behind the deterioration of Zimbabwe-West relations in the post-colonial Africa, the main causative agent is the issue of realization of the continuity of global coloniality and offer an anti-imperial solution to the problem. Mugabeism defined by Ndhlovu-Gatsheni (2006 and 2009) as a philosophy that shapes Mugabe views of the declaration of the anti-imperial wars. The projected relations between Zimbabwe-West adequately described by Walter Rodney (1974) as the main reason that unfolds the story of underdevelopment, whereby colonialism and neo-colonialism deprived the development of the developing countries. North-South Relations (Gunder Frank 1993, Samir Amin 2009, Mignolo, 2013) characterized by the exploitation of the periphery by the core whereby capitalist countries developed their economies at the expense of developing countries. Quinjano (2000) coined it as global coloniality, whereby North-South relations structured in the economic zones, the dichotomy of developed and developed. The realization of the 'post-colonial neocolonized state' (Spivak 2010, Mbembe 2000 and Ndlovu-Gatsheni 2013) created hostilities between Zimbabwe and West, the Western countries wanted to continue to dominate in global affairs through control of world economies envisaged by capitalist-liberal ideology, however Zimbabwe under Mugabe regime crafted policies such as indigenization and land reform to dismantle the global-capitalist tendencies.

"I am still the Hitler of the time, This Hitler has only one objective, justice for his own people, sovereignty for his people, recognition of the independence of his people, and their rights to

133

their resources. If that is Hitler, then let me be Hitler tenfold, ten times that what we stand for" (Mugabe 2003)

From Mugabeism perspective, his policies threatened the outside world and influenced the dynamics of Zimbabwe foreign relations, the issue of preserving sovereignty was the mandatory prognosis of Mugabe regime, realizing the dangers of neocolonialism and put measures. In analysis, the relationship between Zimbabwe and the west deteriorated for political rise that was informed by the conflict of hegemonic interest and anti-imperial interest, clashes to conceive the hostility between the West and Zimbabwe.

More so, the deterioration of Zimbabwe-West relations influenced the dynamics of international politics in the 21st century. The main reason was the political contestation of ideologies, whereby Zimbabwe engaged in the movement of calling for reforming the most controversial global governance headed by the United Nations Security Council (UNSC). This has been posing an extraordinary threat to the United States hegemony, since the multipolarity and balance of power concert in the 21st century is shrouded in mystery (Mearsheimer 2001) and the United States engaged in offensive campaign of creating the unipolar society through influencing the structures of social and political values. Robert Gabriel Mugabe once denounced the global injustices, the inversion of Iraq by United States of America (2001), invasion of Libya by North Atlantic Treaty Organization (NATO), the Cambodia question, operationalization of CIA in Africa and various injustices by the West. According to Blair and Curtis (2009) and Chomsky (2016) United States of America inversion of Iraq was inspired by the national interest rather than the issues of Weapons of Mass Destruction (WMD) and democratization project. Against this issue, it raised hostility since Robert Mugabe denounced the evils of the West publicly in United Nations Summit and various gathering. In 2004, George W Bush stated that the policies of Robert Mugabe posed an extraordinary threat to United States foreign policy, and a decade later Barak Obama repeated the same statement and tightened sanction measures on Zimbabwe. In this regard, the United States project is a history of glory and aligning herself with moral-humanistic values and sloganize democratic-capitalist ideology as global political values, hence Zimbabwe actions towards exposing the nonrealistic politics of the West deteriorated the relations. In this regard, Zimbabwe emerged as the voice of the voiceless, that champion the global reformist paradigm in the international system, hence it attracted few friends from the East and parade of enemies from the West, therefore this is the central reason in understanding Zimbabwe-West hostilities.

The deterioration of Zimbabwe-West relations in post-colonial politics informed by democratic conundrum in the coffers of Zimbabwe body politic, Sachikonye (2011) states that, Zimbabwe embarked on land reform programme as an economic redemptive programme, however at the same time democratic principle was violated, the notion of property rights. The violent occupation of white farms in the year 2002 without compensation violated Britain and Zimbabwe diplomatic agreements at Lancaster house Conference and All Donors Conference in the 1990s. The case of Von Abbo, De Freeth v Republic of Zimbabwe prosecuted by SADC Tribunal rule in favor of white farmers, however due to nature of the international law, whereby it was voluntary and not enforceable (Dugard 2009) the Zimbabwean government refused to implement the judgement and continued land distribution without compensation. This issue led to the sanctioning of Zimbabwe by the European Union through Cotonou Partnership Agreement Article 96 and United States ZIDERA of 2002 (Zimbabwe Democratic Economic Recovery Act), this signalled the deterioration of Zimbabwe-West relations in the 21st century. The Zimbabwean government was accused of being undemocratic by the West, therefore the issue of sanctions were justified. In an attempt to re-engage with the West, Emmerson Mnangagwa administration failed to impress the West due to alledged electoral rigging, 1 August 2018 army killing the civilians and the

135

Internet shutdown and continued killings in January that led to sanctioning again of Zimbabwe. In this regard, the triumph of liberal ideology after the collapse of Union Soviet Socialist Republic (USSR) created the new world order that valued democracy as the best form of government and informed by democratic peace theory proposed by Immanuel Kant in 18th Century, hence Western capitalist engaged in foreign policy campaign of democratizing the world that is evidenced by the collapse of dictatorship in Middle East, Asia, Latin America and Africa (Mearsheimer 2001). In analysis, the failure of the democratic project due to controversial land reforms and alleged political violence from the year 2000 to present deteriorated the relations between the West and Zimbabwe, and led to the sanctions and coercive measure for political reformation in Zimbabwe.

However, social factors also contributed immensely to the disintegration of the relations between Zimbabwe and the West in the 21st Century, manifest in racial lines of sociological schema. For Asante (1991, 2003, 2007) and Mazama (2003), the problem with post-colonial state is it treated the effects of colonialism as only political and economic forgetting the mental effects to the colonized society. Mkandawire (2012) penned an article titled "generation of African scholars" whereby first generation of African scholars' over-exhaust the economic effects of colonialism in a Marxist perspective and failed to understand its mental effects. Ngugi wa Thiongo (1983) proposed the theory of decolonizing the mind, but based it on language and culture, whereby the relegation of native languages to the bottom in public communication created the other and alienated Africans from Africa. This particular conception is a major conceptual issue in understanding the contemporary Zimbabwe-West relations.

"One of the most powerful myths of the twentieth century was the notion that the elimination of colonial administrations amounted to the myth of a 'post-colonial world. The heterogeneous and multiple global structures put in place over a period of 450 years did not evaporate with juridical political decolonization of the periphery over the past 50 years. We continue to live under the same 'colonial power matrix' with juridical-political decolonization we moved from a period of 'global colonialism' to the current period of global coloniality" (Grosfoguel 2007;219).

Ramon Grosfoguel coined the theory of global coloniality, that simply explains the continuity of colonialism, whereby coloniality of being manifests in racial form. The global society lacked the system of heterachies (Kontopolous) but employed hierarchy due to racism. In colonial times, native Africans where ghettoized by the colonialist, that even continue in the post-colonial society and still cherish the idea of inequality. In this regard, the Zimbabwean government embarked on land reform programme as to restore racial power to the black society and dismantle the coloniality of being, whereby the society was structured in dichotomies of rational-irrational, inferior-superior, primitive-civilized and traditional-modern (Quinjano 2000), ghetto and suburbs. In analysis, the relationship between Zimbabwe and the West due to colonialism and post-colonial coloniality exploded into hatred, whereby the social calling for correcting racial imbalances penned the hatred between Zimbabwe and the West.

Conclusion: Mapping the contours of the Future

In conclusion, Zimbabwe-West relations remain the most important issue in the study of global diplomacy and foreign policy. The dynamics of this relations influences the structural shift of global politics and power relations. The relationship between Zimbabwe-West has triple heritage from pre-colonial, colonial and post-colonial, but the central problem was the question of the genuineness of the relations. Realist philosophers, put forward the idea of state interaction in the international system is defined by state interest (survival) and struggle for power. In contrary to realist school of thoughts, idealists believe that post-1945 global society is informed by the ideal of quest for peace and co-operation for peace and developmental purposes. Bridging the gap between these two dominating paradigms of the international relations, dependency theory emerges from the Carribean-Hispanophone society and the global society, defined Africa's underdevelopment as rooted in North-South relations and exploitation by the developed countries. These theories provide a distinctive scholarship paradigm of the central problem of Zimbabwe-West relations that even continue to deteriorate in post-Mugabe era. The main problematic issues discussed in this essay, but mainly 'high politics', play a central role to comprehend the discourses. The issues of land reform, democratic crisis, political call for reforming global politics and imperial blockade has a major effect in deteriorating the relations between Zimbabwe and the West in the 21st Century. The politics of the 21st century, informed by 9/11 attack and the controversial issues of Zimbabwe, however social factors such as dismantling racism fabricated as a result of slavery (William, 2002), colonialism and coloniality created a compositive feature that later exploded as land reform and indigenization policies as the project of decolonization. The new world order politics is not about the end of history or the triumph of liberal-capitalist, it's about issues of creating heterachies, recognizing the small state's sovereignty and their impact in global affairs and the rise of China, creating the hopes of the existence of global multi-polar system.

References
Amin, S. (1990) Delinking, Zed Books
Asante, M.K. (1991) 'The Afrocentricity Idea in Education", Journal of Negro Education
Asante, M.K. (2003) Afrocentricity; The Theory of Social Change, Illinois; African American Images

Asante, M.K. (2007) An Afrocentric Manifesto; Cambridge; Polity Press

Fanon, F. (1963) The Wretched of the Earth, Paris; Penguin

Grosfoguel, R. (2007) The Epistemic Decolonial Turn; Towards Global Political Economy; Duke University Press.

Gunder Frank, A. (1984) Critique and Anti-Critique; Essays on Dependency and Reformism, London; Macmillan

Mahomva, R.R. (2016) Chimurenga Culture in Contemporary Society, Bulawayo; Leaders of Africa Network;

Mandani, M. (1998) Citizen and the Subject; Contemporary Africa and the Legacy of Late Colonialism; Kampala; Makerere University

Mazama, A. ed(2003) The Afrocentric Paradigm, Trenton; Africa World Press

Mazrui, A. (2002) Africanity Redefined, Chicago; Chicago university Press

Mignolo, W.D. (2011) The darker Side of Western Modernity; Global Futures, Decolonial Options, Durham; Duke University Press.

Mkandawire, T. (2013) Three Generations of African Scholars

Muchemwa, T. (2012) Struggle for Land in Zimbabwe from 1966-2010, Harare; Heritage Publishers

Mtizira, N. (2008) The Chimurenga Protocol, Harare; Weaver Press

Ndlovu-Gatsheni, S.J. (2009) Do Zimbabwe Exist? Trajectories of Nationalism, National Identity Formation and Crisis in Post-Colonial State, Peter Lang

Ndlovu-Gatsheni, S.J. (2013) Coloniality of Power in Post-Colonial Africa; Myths of Decolonization, Dakar; CODESERIA

Ndlovu-Gatsheni, S.J. (2015) Mugabeism? History, Politics and Power in Zimbabwe, London; Palgrave Macmillan

Ngugi wa Thiongo. (1981) decolonizing the Mind, Politics of Language in Africa, New York; Heinemann

Nyawo, V.Z. (2012) Dilemmas of Agrarian Reform in Independent Zimbabwe and South Africa, Gweru; Mambo Press

William, C. (1992) Destruction of Black Civilization; Chicago; Chicago University Press.

Quinjano, A. (2000) Coloniality of Power and Eurocentrism in Latin America, International Sociology, volume 15 (2) pp215-232

Sachikonye, L. (2011) When a State Turns of Its Citizens. Institutionalized Violence and Political Culture, Harare; Weaver Press

Spivak, G. C. (1994) Can Subaltern Speak, Delhi; Stefan Nowotny Publishers

Innovative Storytelling and the Future of Shona Folktales in Zimbabwe: A Study of Ignatius Mabasa's tales.

Tinashe Muchuri
Zimbabwe Open University

ABSTRACT

*I*ndigenous Knowledge Systems comprise of the bodies of knowledge created by the ancestors in Africa as footprints through which the present and future generations are able to see the future. Storytelling has been lagging behind though it is a major part of the Shona society's moral, ethical, knowledge builder, and entertainment. Of late an upsurge of storytellers moving away from telling stories around fires during the night is increasing. Due to the change of times storytellers are following children wherever they are. Some scholars underplay the role being played by Ignatius Mabasa in developing storytelling and in mapping the Shona folklore future in Zimbabwe. This chapter critically examined Mabasa's innovative storytelling approach in the 21ˢᵗ century as a performer and contemporary' Shona folklore writer. Furthermore, the chapter investigated whether new storytelling techniques are making the Shona folklore relevant, competing with new technological advancement; interrogated the forms that Mabasa's tales are created in, challenges encountered in the creation process and in marketing concept and how the creator overcomes the impedance. Moreso the chapter looked at sustainability of Mabasa's innovative ideas and the milestones made or opportunities that can be exploited in sustaining storytelling in Zimbabwe and Africa at large. Employing Critical Discourse Analysis theory the paper utilized a descriptive content analysis approach of Mabasa's two tales to identify innovative traits that promote Shona storytelling sustainability. While appreciating Mabasa's creativity and dedication to innovative storytelling the paper interrogated the supposition behind the portrayal of Baboon and Hare characters in modern costumes and utilizing modern props viewed by cultural conservationists as harmful*

to indigenous cultural practices. It therefore attempted to deeper questions about the posterity of indigenous knowledge systems in order to promote innovation and sustainability of storytelling in Shona relevant to the contemporary society.
Key words: Innovation, Indigenous Knowledge Systems, Sustainable Storytelling.

INTRODUCTION

According to World Book Dictionary (1992) refer innovation as 'a change made in the established way of doing things' and Oxford Advanced Learner's Dictionary (2010) defines innovation as 'the introduction of new things, ideas, or ways of doing things.' I also add that innovation is a disruptive force that changes, improves, or distorts the status quo or reshape old ideas in order to make them adapt to new spaces, time, and location, technology and that to be innovative is to be adventurous, to be brave, to be committed, to be confident, to be dedicated, to be determined to face challenges with a new thought or a revamped thought regardless of risks envisioned or discouragements along the way in order to achieve a goal of easy of doing things.

Indigenous is a belonging to a particular place rather than coming from somewhere (Oxford Advanced Learner's Dictionary, 2010) else hence indigenous knowledge systems are bodies of knowledge created by the ancestors as footprints through which the present and future generations are able to pass insights, wisdom, ideas and perceptions and the history from one generation to the next generation.

Storytelling is a way of recording and expressing one's feelings and attitudes as responses to what one experienced around one's environment (Gbadegesin, 1984) and retelling it to a single listener or more through voice and gestures (Ngugi, 1986).

Learning Shona enhances imagination and strengthens critical understanding of issues (Mufanechiya and Mufanechiya, 2015:43) and Grant (1989) avers that children taught culture in their languages appreciate stories of own country more and probably contribute to the stories when grown up, constructing a rational and reasonable person in their relationship with nature and other human beings.

African storytelling is attributed to construct, uphold good social order and as a way of passing on traditions, codes and values (Vambe. 2001) explaining natural phenomena, teaching morality, provide African people with a sense of identity, entertainment of the community (Ngugi wa Thiong'o 1982). Storytelling enhances thinking, expand knowledge, community building and develop public speaking skills (Mabasa, 2014).

This essay highlights milestones achieved by Mabasa's storytelling innovation and opportunities laid bare in print, audio, online or visual motivating listeners to be willing participants and creators.

Storytelling is a proven solid early childhood development tool that premised on in the past and has become critical during Zimbabwe's updated curriculum overhaul based on the Nziramasanga commission report (1999).

In the past storytelling by parents, grandparents, aunts, uncles and children learning to become part of the storytelling community was a common learning institute. Modern education systems shifted Shona storytelling as it borrows from other knowledge systems in what the Shona say, 'ideas are like fire, they are borrowed (Mazano moto anogokwa) laying bare that Shona knowledge systems were ever in motion in recording of history, bringing and inspiring new ideas attesting to what Obioha (2015) and Vambe (2001) posit that, "No culture can claim absolute sufficiency. There is something every culture lacks but which it needs" and that Storytelling is a rich repository of norms, morals and values, celebration, warning, mourning or entertainment.

Mabasa (2019) adds that Storytellers create stories not from the blue but are usually influenced by their society answering to the assertion that says, best writers are those who write about their environment. In the Shona context Mabasa has made great strides towards innovation and sustainability of storytelling through adapting new technologies and the changing firesides.

Zimunya (2018)'s assertion that 'if you marginalize a language, you marginalize a people' as a response to the proclamation and recognisation of 16 local languages in the Constitution of Zimbabwe (Act No.20) 2013 without putting mechanism through which these languages would be used and learned. The embracing of storytelling by the updated primary and secondary education curriculum, United Nations (UN) promulgation of 2019 as a year of indigenous languages, the outcry by 2013 ZIBF Writers Workshop attendees denouncing Mabasa's Redhiyo yaTsuro as a rebellious attempt by a language dissident to destroy Shona knowledge systems as a reflection of the changing firesides informs the need for this chapter.

United Nations General Assembly dedicated the year 2019 as The International Year of Indigenous Languages focusing at the marginalized languages of the people from Polar Circles, Arabian Peninsula, Australia, East Asia and Central America and was celebrated as a way of raising awareness of critical risks these languages face and their value as medium of culture, knowledge systems and ways of life. UN has seen that indigenous languages are an investment in spearheading their communities' destinies as well as participating in their country's economic, cultural, and political life; providing 'unique systems and understanding of the world, sustainable development, peace building and reconciliation, fundamental human rights and freedoms for indigenous peoples, social inclusiveness, literacy, poverty reduction and international cooperation, cultural values, diversity and heritage.'

This chapter concurs with the adage that, change is not easy to embrace as Mabasa's innovative Shona storytelling encountered a stiff societal repudiations and brickbats as conservationists argue that they cannot allow their Baboon and Hare stories to be mutilated and decimated by contemporaries instead the contemporaries should use other characters for their stories not their beloved Gudo naTsuro. Mabasa (2013) at the ZIBF Writers Workshop held at the National Gallery of Zimbabwe was labelled cultural sinner who needs deliverance, a rebel and irresponsible cultural dissident masquerading as a writer and storyteller and a mischief taking folktales to new technologies and give characters modern props (Mabasa 2014). Wasamba weighs him down arguing that taking folklore to new technologies is a mischief and making Tsuro slove modern things defile folktales.

Mabasa(2014) further contends that, "Folktales should be made exciting and relevant so that our children today do not lose interest in that heritage just because it is not responding to social change

In addition Mabasa (2014) argues that learners are moulded around being pragmatic against theoretic hence the call for innovative ideas to secure storytelling sustainability. However, this has created the impression that the new storytellers are mutating indigenous knowledge systems for the benefiting imperialistic views. Conservationist demanded that every storyteller involving Tsuro naGudo should follow the structure, the settings and use props that were used in the ancient storytelling sessions implying that Hare and Baboon stories should not move with times. Yet Shona ancestors assert that, '**Kare haagari ari kare**' and '**Gore harizi pakaza rimwe**' or '**Chinokura chinokotama musoro wegudo chava chinokoro**' an admission that life changes, everything changes and therefore change must be embraced relevantly and storytellers should thus follow the changing firesides in order to sustain Shona storytelling and be able to solve current poblems.

Mushava (2016, 2019) describes Mabasa as a 'disruptive innovator of the Shona novel'. Mabasa is indeed a disciple of the Shona wisdom which embraces change. Muyambo (2016) attests that Mabasa followed the dictates of the Shona tradition of embracing change and move with times. However this chapter discovers that Mabasa is among other innovators who maybe by fate fell on the wayside after being attacked by the Shona language conservationists. There is a time when Tsuro and Gudo were recorded jumping fences to steal milk at a farm and also stole sacks of orange. There is also a time when Tsuro was recorded as farmers together with Gudo and animals like Nzou and Mhembwe. Hassan Musa together with the Literature Bureau tried to bring the story into the city with the publication of Hassan Musa comic books. Mbuya Tendai Makura weighed in with her Zimbabwe Children's Literature Foundation which published quite a number of folktales which were a rendition of tales children grew up hearing from their parents and grandparents but were coming in hard copies and some accompanied with audio cassettes. The Zimbabwe Children's Literature Foundation published Gombiro (1985) Tsuro in 'Tsuro Kanoshereketa' where Tsuro went on a journey meeting people digging for mice without a hoe that he lent his hoe '**Ndinoda mukaka wangu. Kana musina motondiripa nebadza iro**' and he was given the hoe. He also met people constructing a road and eating sadza with mufushwa and offered them his mice on condition they eat the mice and serve him with soup. They could not honour their promise. They compensated him with a gun which he later gave to a king who wanted to scare away pigs which were destroying his fields. The king broke the gun and compensated him with a beautiful girl Runako and speaks of her as someone whom he cannot give to anyone because he wants her to brew him tea rich in milk. *"Kuseka zvangu mukoma wangu uyu mukadzi wangu, ndinoda kuti anobika tii hobvu kumba* *kwangu'*. Throughout this tale only props have changed but everything else remained the same in what Mabasa (2014) argues,

Tsuro's wit and tricks should not be confined to the old ... our Tsuro just like our changing lifestyles should also adapt or else he will die because he will lose relevance. It is not only Tsuro's setting that needs an overhaul, but his language also, yet returning those hunhu/ubuntu values we hold dear and that hold us together as a people (Mabasa, 2014).

Thereby concurring with Gbadegesin (1984) who says storytelling is a recording and expressing of one's feelings and attitudes as responses to what one experienced around one's environment. It is unfortunate that though Gombiro is one of the innovators of the Shona Folktales he suffered the writer of one story syndrome.

Tsuro naGudo story stayed in confines of the farms, bush and the rural areas until Mabasa emerged with innovative ideas of telling it using modern props, settings like the urban areas and depicting the lives of modern people living in the urban areas and giving Baboon and Hare the power to acquire modern utility products as those used in today's civilized world and also utilizing many available mediums through which these tales can be accessed by the audience.

KUWANDA HUUYA KWAKARAMBWA NEMUROYI

Shona knowledge systems accept and appreciate migrants into its territories. There are stories and monuments constructed by the Shona people but with time many things happened and names of certain places changed to new historical names. In ancient Shona society there were places like Manyanga, Matonjeni, Dzimbabwe and Dungwiza now by these new names Ntabazinduna, Matopos, Great Zimbabwe and Chitungwiza respectively? Why then should the story remain stagnant without being relevant to this day when proverbs show that Shona knowledge systems embrace diversity. In Redhiyo yaTsuro, Shumba tells Tsuro to return the gadget where he had found it. Shumba's and Nzou's act can be referred to as the act of conservationists denying innovation in storytelling.

147

RUZIVO MOTO UNOGOKWA

Shona knowledge systems encourage borrowing of ideas and are very clear on what should be borrowed and how it should be borrowed. Ideas should be borrowed, but should be tested, measured according to Shona knowledge before using then. Hence **zano pangwa une rakowo**. Since the Shona borrows, there is agreement that knowledge is not stagnant but flows like spring water which continues bringing out fresh and refreshing water. Shumba and other animals in Redhiyo yaTsuro interrogated Tsuro's watch idea that he brought into the jungle. They found it useless and not relevant in the bush hence returning it to the storekeeper for swap and top. A modern day business concept in the informal computer and mobile phone business In Redhiyo yaTsuro, Tsuro tells Kamba that a radio transmit local and international news (**inotaura nyaya dzemuno nedzekunze**) and that was the reason why he had brought the radio into their territory so that he could be aware of what is happening in the other worlds. Tsuro alludes to globalisation. He wanted to be a global citizen. Furthermore the Shona says, **Kugara nhaka huona dzevamwe** -We copy from others for us to use our heritage well. Stagnant water is a source of dangerous water borne diseases such as malaria, diarrhoea, typhoid, cholera hence ideas that remain idle and constant is a breeding space for failure. Flowing water is safe except it is polluted from the source or from its tributaries hence Shona people should be aware of what they accept therefore **zano pangwa une rako** (receive advice benchmarking with your own).

For foreigners and their ideas to say, they should be agreeing with Shona values are good and if not they are thrown away. Ideas only co-habit if they agree. It is hard to live together without mutual understanding, hence in Redhiyo yaTsuro, when all the animals refused to let Tsuro stay with the watch, he went back to the storekeeper to do as swap and top for a radio. When Tsuro failed to make peace with others in the jungle he did the only noble thing according to Shona

148

knowledge system, to make peace with others by asking for forgiveness. **Kugara kunzwana**, Tsuro says, "I am sorry my friends, I wanted to get news about other places and also to get entertained by the music **(Ndiregereiwo shamwari dzangu, ndanga ndichidawo kuziva zvinhu zvinoitika kune dzimwe nzvimbo pamwe chete nekunakidzwa nemagitare.)**

KUKANYA HURANGANA
Mabasa mainly tell stories in Shona and sometimes code switches to English as matter of accommodating non-Shona speaking audience complies with the proverb **kugara hunzwana**, that encourages people to live together and only if they understand one another. Ngugi wa Thiongo in *Decolonising the mind* (1987) alludes to the importance of using one's language when expressing important ideas that impact the African community. In Redhiyo yaTsuro, Tsuro buys a watch that he uses to measure time needed to do each activity. Tsuro took his watch around, showing off to relatives. Other animals refused to entertain Tsuro's watch, his idea was not accommodated. It had no takers. In a Shona village, you have to consult first before implementation. Tsuro brought new ideas because he was the most travelled person in their society but those who stayed behind did not blindly accept his borrowed ideas without censoring it. The society has a way of taking in innovative ideas that are good and healthy for its development. This exposes the democratic side of the Shona society because for every decision is after consultation and interrogation. Once the idea is found to be good it sails through making the Shona being socially inclusive. In Redhiyo yaTsuro, Tsuro acted without consulting the other citizens of the jungle hence he found himself isolated. Tsuro was troubled a lot. He sat on top of a rock and switched off the radio **(Tsuro kanetseka kwazvo. Akagara Padombo, achibva adzima redhiyo yake).'** He did self evaluation decided how to mend his ways with everyone, He decided to consult Kamba whom he persuaded to intermediate between him and the rest of the jungle citizens. When

149

Kamba asked him what is the thing that was making the noise, Tsuro answers that, "It is technology Kamba ... Technology is moving with times (**Inonzi tekinoroji Kamba! ... Tekinoroji ndiko kufambirana nenguva**)." Mabasa expresses that, a people who doesn't accept change and innovation dies, concurring with Shona saying that says **gore harizi pakaza rimwe** (Years are not the same, they change).

However as innovative ideas stir our thinking; people should remember Shona wise counsel that **Mvura bvongodzi ndiyo garani**. Innovative ideas unsettles the status quo, it changes the way things were being done, it unravels some furs, but eventually everything settles down and the community celebrates with the innovator and true to Mabasa's words that:

Our problem is in wasting time in lamenting that we are not given space to express ourselves, on the internet, or on many platforms in the world, and if you ask them what they are doing they tell you things are hard and I as a person in the field of writing has taken upon myself to write the tales, to help preserve them. (Mabasa. 2014)

Fortune (1982) asserts that storytelling by parents is more concerned with planting and maintaining discipline and attitudes in their children and that by grandparents' aims at correcting misdeeds. In Kunene (1991), he concurs that lessons derived from African stories teach children about moralities by giving them a sense of belonging and indentify. In Chipo neChipopai, Chipo meets Chipopai eating the pie. For parents to correct their children it means they should be continuously monitoring their children's daily activities making the issues contemporary, therefore there is need for storytellers to strive to be relevant to their current situation by telling appropriate stories hence Mabasa argues that he is not reinventing the wheel because even in the past there is a Shona tale of Gudo naTsuro tales used technologies of their contemporary times. It concurs with Ngugi

(1982) assertion that borrows props and developments in keeping the people's history alive.

Today, Mabasa is his audiences' darling; was engaged by the First Lady Amai Auxilia Mnangagwa to be part of Amai neNgano, Star Fm for Ngano programme, and NGOs to write tales that help create awareness on different phenomena.

IMBWA INOROVERWA PACHINYIRO

Chipo neChipopai is a short tale yet packed with meaning. It is among what Fortune categorised as tales told by parents to instil corrective behaviour in their children. Though it is in Shona, Chipo neChipopai is dealing with global topical themes of early child marriages and children sexual abuse. Mabasa places the community in a Kombi that included activists who know about child rights and who understand the power of citizen's arrest that can be effected on child abusers and other offenders before handing them over to police law to take its course. The activists in the kombi did not wait long to arrest Chipopai because Shona knowledge systems advise that time does not wait for anyone (**Nguva haimirire munhu**) and also that a dog must be punished at the crime scene (**imbwa inoroverwa pachinyiro**). Chipopai tried to run away but was caught and brought before the court of law where he was sentenced to spent a long time in the prison. Here, Mabasa brings children to the things they are familiar with and things they love to have but used as baits used by their abusers. Children know that ice cream is bought in supermarkets and thus Chipo and Chipopai go to the supermarket to buy the ice cream. These are children's lived experiences and environments that will lure them to the story as the storyteller narrates the events. Mabasa is therefore not running away from the dictates of knowledge systems but evolves within the confines of Shona knowledge systems innovatively by modernizing the tale bringing in new technology for easy accessibility by modern audiences on WhatsApp, Youtube, Facebook and Google search. He is simply following the changing firesides which are now found on television, radio, online, and mobile phones. The act by Zimbabwe's Ministry of Primary and Secondary Education to approve tales use in schools is a refreshing and innovative milestone that brings the people together to discuss topical issues in a short time. The commuters therefore contest the assertions that say 'there is no hurry in Africa' and that 'Africans lack urgency'.

REGAI DZIVE SHIRI MAZAI HAANA MUTO
Chipo neChipopai fits well with the proverb, 'let them be birds, eggs have no soup; (regai dzive shiri mazai haana muto). There is no record of people being imprisoned or punished for abusing children to the level it has been now. Mabasa moved with times as Chipo naChipopai criminalizes early marriage as opposed to the past's moral grounding where instead of criminalizing the abuser, the parents would demand payment of lobola. Mabasa shows that change can be achieved without moving away from self but just reorient one's past in order to fit in the demands of the modern fast society. Short tales find its way easy on radio and television programmes as fillers. After unsettling the longer narratives, Mabasa's short versions like the Tshaka's assegai has find its takers as the Ministry of Primary and Secondary education has approved some of his tales to be used in the curriculum. On 25 May 2019 Mabasa was telling the African diplomatic community stories as they commemorated Africa Day. Mabasa (2019) posits that storytelling helps people to understand different society's myriad phenomena and challenges and how such can be solved;

Perhaps children are seeing action films with fighting people where they are killing each other with guns which doesn't help. We grew up knowing that, a young one of a leopard is the one which grew up fighting. In Tales, fights are there but they are solved amicably allowing the society to move on and also helping children to learn how to solve their differences. Thus, ngano gives people a room for dialogue to solve their differences. (Mabasa, 2019)

PANORAIRWA MWANA WASHE MURANDA TERERA

This Shona proverb urges servants to listen carefully of the good ideas that the king says to his children. Everyone benefits from that wisdom and can be used to strengthen relations and sustain it through appreciation of **diverse cultural values and identities**. Shona people have relatives and friends in the Diaspora who may bring new ideas which can be used to easy challenges through importation of goods and ideas or just the direct financial investment like the homelink initiatives that the country has embraced in order to develop the country. However not all ideas from outside home are good as innovation may also bring bad results as seen by the expensive cars, second hand cars which pollute theair space hence Tsuro in Redhiyo yaTsuro, said. "I heard nothing as I was coming from where the people live **(Handina chandanzwa nekuti kunogara vanhu ndiko kwandanga ndiri)."**

NGANO ZHINJI DZINOTANGA PANOPERERA SARUNGANO

Fortune (1982) said story endings reveal how adaptive tales are. Story tellers ends the tales with, "**Ndipo pakaperera sarungano** (That is where the storyteller ended), **Ndipo pakafira sarungano** (And then the storyteller died), **Ndipo pakagumira Sarungano** (That is where the storyteller ended), **Ndipo pakamwira nhondwa sarungano** (That is where the storyteller choked and died by drowning), **Ndiko kufa kwasara rungano** (And so they died and the story remained). Mabasa (2019) extends where Fortune ended on the discussion about tale endings positing that it is the Sarungano who dies but story remains, Furthermore arguing that this allows the new storyteller to look around on what issues need to be addressed so that they can be the new sources of the tale relevant to the new generation in order to address the challenges in real time. Mabasa's assertion set the new storyteller on an innovative threshold demanding the new storyteller to fit into the life of the particular generation, using the available technology, recording new developments in the community in which the story or issues are to be stored or tackled. The researcher also notes that the old tales are the footprints which provides the new storyteller with the framework and structure of a folktale but still for the student to be relevant, one should find their new footing by branching out of the forerunners shaping their own and following the new dreams as demanded by their situation as they actively participate in learning important aspects of their culture (Ngugi wa Thiong'o 1987). This flexibility in Shona storytelling therefore allows audience to actively participate as backing vocalists or in form of asking questions that the storyteller answers or throws back to the audience to answer thereby disrupting the storytelling process in both time and the structure of the tale depending on the audience to which the story is being told to.

IMPLICATIONS

Folktales are an act of showing bravery, where the little expected results shock the most expected results. It is the chronicles of how giant ideas like Goliath are slain by the small David mighty ideas. Tales can be said to be documentation of events of their time that were recorded orally by our ancestors hence Mabasa refer to them as newspapers of the time they were told of the events that would have happened and as a result some stories died because they were not timeless but others survived because they were timeless. In this regard, most hard news stories survive only the day they are published but deeply analyzed feature stories survive generations after generations hence the relationship of Gudo and Tsuro in Shona tales is like deeply analyzed stories that can fit in every situation in any generation. This is qualified by storytelling functions of mediating and transmitting of knowledge and information about culture, world views morals, values, norms, and what the future is expected to be (Ngugi wa Thiong'o 1982). Not to say that all feature stories that find space in the new generation are relevant to these times without reorientation, Mabasa's argument that storytelling was like a newspaper holds water as it speak along innovative ideas therefore immediately correct the misbehaviour of the people in the community in which they were told,. And a newspaper is regarded as a primary source for a people's history. So, tales were also used to record our historical events that would have changed the people's way of life in what Chinyowa (2001) attests that storytelling is a way beyond just a source of pleasure, the story aids in sharpening the people's creativity and imagination, shaping their way of presenting themselves before others, training their intellect and regulating their emotions, attitudes and feelings.

Through most of his tales, Mabassa oozes with innovative ideas that conserve the structure of storytelling skills and indigenous values and norms. His tales is a clear demonstration that Shona knowledge moves with times and document contemporary developments. Mabasa (2014) argues that if the same tales were used in the past to solve societal problems what can surely stop them from solving our myriad problems today?

If we put Tsuro naGudo in silos, we risk presenting them as they were in the time of Mbuya Nehanda and our children will not find them appealing. If we really cared about Tsuro naGudo, we would be rebranding them so that they are relevant to young people today. (Mabasa, 2014).

In all his efforts Mabasa (2019) wants to bring back the shona people to their right senses or to where Achebe said 'where the hail stone started hitting us' and find the way out of the problems facing them hence he says;

Tales are not mere stories but they inspire you to think, they give you knowledge, they give you an understanding of expected morals in your society and how to live well with others in your community, they teach you to be a storyteller, they give you confidence to speak before a people, away from an individual worlds that we have constructed for ourselves in our ears through earphones that deprives us of conversations. So it is an effort to bring back people together again reminding

155

them that a person is a person because of others around them not because of their electronic gadgets. (Mabasa, 2019)

CONCLUSION AND RECOMMENDATIONS

This study found out that Shona storytelling always moves with times, it has never been static as is proven by various proverbs which point to the urgency of the Shona people in its desire to move with times. Mabasa's critics therefore are hugging kusafunga as they seem to ignore the urgency in Shona knowledge systems' urge and instruction to move with times, be innovative and embrace change. Mabasa has managed to adapt to changing firesides through his embrace of the new technology in his bid to find audiences where they socialise in this fast moving life of this modern day. Shona indigenous knowledge systems therefore have ever been supporting innovative ideas as a way of sustaining the development of storytelling hence Mabasa is therefore not a sinner. Mabasa is not an irresponsible cultural dissident. Mabasa is not a rebel bent on mutilating Shona indigenous knowledge systems but a loyal Shona cultural ambassador taking Shona to the world the same way Tuku took Korekore to the world through Music. Mabasa is a faithful innovator of the Shona language whose aim is to prevent Shona storytelling from disappearing. Mabasa has taken upon himself to not only talk about the innovative use of storytelling in solving our contemporary challenges but has gone further into putting to practice by leading the way in showing what should be done with Shona indigenous knowledge systems. Mabasa is not just a speaker but a doer whose hunger for the preservation of Shona language extends the same journeys, paths capturing new territories that the ancestors because of change of eras did not traverse. Instead of vilifying him Shona knowledge conservationists should embrace him and complement his efforts to take Shona storytelling to the global sphere. Mabasa's innovative skills saw him attending the Third Razavi International Storytelling Festival in Iran as far back as 2012. What this means is that his stories has been seen speaking to the people of this time's needs locally, regionally and internationally therefore they are relevant and thus sustainable. Moreover this chapter has observed that, Shona storytelling is a long life travel by a bus that the old storytellers disembark upon arriving at their destinations as the bus is filled by new storytellers who also disembark when they reach their destination and leave their seats to yet another generation of storytellers thereby illustrating that Shona knowledge systems encourage urgency, embrace change, advocate for change, borrow ideas therefore it is not stagnant but a flowing river being strengthened by its tributaries.

However this study observed a noticeable increase in the utilisation of indigenous foodstuffs in the modern day, increased campaigns to utilise indigenous diseases fighting and prevention methods, consumption of indigenous foods, growing of indigenous grains and as a way of mitigating the effects of climate change and non-communicable diseases therefore it recommends that since masawu, tsvubvu, mazhanje, nyii, mutetenerwa, and mahewu have found their way into the modern market system, storytelling should take them aboard in order to sustain their effects on the Shona society's health.

References:
Achebe, C. (1958). *Things Fall Apart*. Nigeria: William Heinemann Ltd.
Barnhart, C. L. and Barnhart, R. K. (1992) *World Book Dictionary*. Chicago: World Book, Inc.
Chinyowa, K. (2001). *"The Sarungano and Shona Storytelling: an African Theatrical Paradigm." Studies in*
Theatre and Performance **21**(1): 18-30.
Constitution of Zimbabwe Amendment (No.20) 2013.
Dalton, M. and Stockil, C. (1987) Shangani Folk Tales. Harare:Longman.
Fortune, G. (1982) *Ngano Volume 11,* (collected by Mufuka, R 1972 & Edt Fortune), Mercury Press:
        Harare

-----------------------(2010) *Oxford Advanced Learner's Dictionary.* New York: Oxford University Press.

Gbadegesin, S. (1984). *"Destiny, personality and the ultimate reality of human existence."* Ultimate Reality
and Meaning **7**(3): 173-188.

Gombiro, P. (1985) *Tsuro Kanoshereketa.* Harare: Zimbabwe Children's Literature Foundation (ZCLF).

Grant, M. (1989). *School methods with younger children.* London: Evans Brothers Ltd.

Kunene, D. P. (1991). *Journey in the African epic.* Research in African Literatures **22** (2): 205-223.

Mabasa, I. T. (2013) *Redhiyo yaTsuro.* Harare: Bhabhu Books.

Mabasa, I, T. (2013) *Behind my children's stories.* Harare: Zimbabwe International Book Fair

Mabasa, I. T. (2014) *Language teaching, the cultural dissident.* The Herald. Harare: Zimpapers. 29 July, 2014

Mabasa, I. T. (2016) *Chipo neChipopayi.* Harare: Bhabhu Books.

Mabasa, I. T. Mabasa releases folk tales. The Herald. Zimpapers. 17 April, 2017.

Mabasa, I. T. (2019) *Sarungano Ignatius Tirivangani Mabasa vanotandara naTinashe Muchuri vachitaura ngano.* munyori.com.

Mbara, V. (2017) Mabasa releases folk tales. The Herald. Harare: Zimpapers. 17 April, 2017.

Mkandla, P.N. (1974) *Abaseguswini lezothamlilo.* Harare: Longman Zimbabwe (Pvt) Ltd.

Mufanechiya, T. & Mufanechiya, A. (2015) *Teaching Chishona in Zimbabwe: A Curriculum Analysis Approach.* In The Journal of Pan African Studies, vol.8, no.8, November 2015. Masvingo: Great Zimbabwe University

Mungoshi, C. (1989) *Stories from a Shona Childhood.* Harare: Baobab Books (a division of Academic Books (Pvt) Ltd)

Mungoshi, C. (1991) *One Day, Long Ago: More Stories from a Shona Childhood*. Harare: Baobab Books (a division of Academic Books (Pvt) Ltd)

Mushava, S. (2016) *Masters and disruptive innovators*. The Herald. Harare:Zimpapers

Mushava, S. (2019) *Prison officer's runaway imagination*. The Herald. Harare:Zimpapers.

Muyambo (2016) *Indigenous Knowledge Systems: An Alternative for Mitigating HIV and AIDS in Zimbabwe*. Harare: *Alternation 23,2 (2016) 289 – 308* ISSN 1023-1757

Ngugi wa Thiong'o (1982). *Devil on the Cross (English translation of Caitaani mutharaba-Ini)*. Nairobi, Kenya, Heinemann Educational Books (East Africa) Ltd 1980.

Ngugi wa Thiong'o (1987). *Decolonising the Mind: The Politics of Language in African Literature*. Harare: Zimbabwe Publishing House (ZPH).

Vambe., M. T. (2001). *Orality and Cultural Indentities in Zimbabwe*. Gweru, Zimbabwe: Mambo Press.

Wasamba, P. (2018) *A ZIBF Indaba with a difference*. Harare. The Patriot. The Heritage.

UNESCO. (2019) International *Year of indigenous languages 2019*. Official website for the International Year: https://en.iyil2019.org/ accessed on 19 June 2019.

Zimbabwereads (2012) *Ignatius Mabasa to go to Third Razavi International Storytelling Festival in Iran*. https://zimbabwereads.org/news/ accessed on 15 May 2019

Reject or Accept Everything

Tendai Rinos Mwanaka

The only route to real freedom or the truth is to accept everything or to reject everything. Reject you know everything, reject there is a God, reject all religions, reject love, reject everything like an atheist, but go beyond atheism and reject yourself. Come to nothingness. That's the truth zone, that's true freedom. I didn't say come to sad nihilism (I didn't say delete yourself). After all everything is an opinion. Just because the majority have enforced it as the truth doesn't mean it's not an opinion. Go back and find out where it all started. It was an opinion. Even mathematically speaking there are instances where 1 plus 1 doesn't equate to 2. The truth is we adapt, we evolve, we live (survive). We are never sure. That's why systems decay and new systems come up to build on previous systems that have run their course and failed to stay the test of time. We are just instances in time, fractured pieces flying and winnowing in time's vastness

Or we can alternatively (or at parallel) accept everything. Accept there is a God, Accept heavens and earth, accept there is love, accept the human condition, and accept your religion and every other religion. Accept he is gay, accept he has children, and accept he doesn't want to get married, accept your nothingness. If you only think just because you are a Catholic and that its the only true religion. If you think you are a Judaist and that its the only true religion, if you think you are a Buddhist and that its the only true religion, you are a liar. That's not true or it's just a sad half-truth. The moment you believe that religion of yours as the truth believe every other religion as the truth, accept everything. Why would you dispute the same God's creations or different Gods' creations. He never created a single thing before so why do you want to think your religion alone is the only one true. I know you can commandeer God and go about dictating what he said or did not say and call it the truth, but the only true god is the Truth, and the only truth is everything or nothing

Dust eventually turned into a golden haze....!
Chipo Martha Bute

What was supposed to be five years of marriage turned out to some sort of informal, yet sanctioned imprisonment. Ray traumatized my emotions and left an irreparable damage in my life. Fear engulfed me and consumed the better part of me until all hope of recuperation faded away. However, the latter proved me wrong!

Ray and I met in 2010 just before his 30th birthday and we fell in love like teenagers. His unconditional love swept me off my feet and I was convinced to marry him at once. I felt so happy in becoming his wife. Holding a marriage certificate was a great achievement to me since I was a school drop-out who held no other valuable certificate besides my birth certificate, of course. Little had I known of the sourness embedded on my so called achievement certificate?

Young as I was, I portrayed a mature attitude. I quickly adapted my life to his and made incessant efforts in pursuit of making our marriage a fulfilling one. I was calm and composed, subservient, a good conversationalist, courteous and respectful to him. On the contrary, my husband had this sneaky behavior I did not understand. He became so manipulative and always wanted things to be done his way. Ray never took any advice from me no-matter how factual they might have been. He kept reminding me of my illiteracy and how primitive I was in dropping out of school.

It was not long before I learnt of his alcoholism and his illicit affairs with other women within the same community with us. He would lie about everything if I happen to ask him. Ray had developed into a pathetic liar. I vividly remember a day when he slapped my face after I showed him a letter from one of his mistresses whom he said was his long forgotten aunt. Each day had its episode and it never got any better.

His drinking became the focus of our daily conversations. I asked him why he was acting that way and he plainly told me that he was trying to get rid of some depression. *'What depression, what pressure when we were just supposed to enjoy our union"!* Before I could comprehend what he said, he went on to tell me of how his family despised me. He said they never liked me from the beginning and they preferred a learned woman to me. His words never moved me anyway, I was not ready to quit. I had to fight for my marriage and I was bold about it. The only thing that was worrisome to me was the fact that I was taking forever to conceive. More often we discussed about this and it would end up with me blinding my eyes with tears.

Two years went by and things got stranger. Ray started seeing another woman who was a fellow school teacher at his. Their love blossomed and she got pregnant for him. Sue bore him a son and news broke all over the community. Some vainly called me a *barren desert* and some teased me. This withered down my confidence and I started dying within. Ray never regretted his actions instead he cautioned me to live by it or leave his house, our house. There was no remorse in his tone. It surprised me. *What had become of Ray, was I losing him just like that?* I wondered.

I was not prepared to take any of his options. I did not want to share him with anyone. I loved him unconditionally; I had undying love for him beneath all frustrations. This made me ignore hints that my reality was a sham. I hoped for change and kept promising myself that one day he would come back to his rightful senses and we would retain our young love.

Gradually my relationship with Ray became dysfunctional. He never bothered taking care of me neither treating me as his wife. We fought over small things and he would insult me even in public. Suddenly my world became a blur, I felt all strength ebb from me. I was no different from a broken cistern that holds no water. It was no lie that I had no value to Ray and his life. Sue had became his primary source of peace, happiness and contentment. *So why did he marry me when he did not love me, why was he priding in making me suffer?* My barrage of questions remained unanswered.

Ray brought Sue into our matrimonial home. This time, all hell broke loose. It was too much to bear and accept. Tension grew between the three of us and perennial arguments dominated our house. Our once beautiful home had now turned into a harbor of drama and chaos. Arrogantly, Sue insulted me and my husband would do nothing about it. I endured all the pain regardless of how much faith I had in re-building my broken marriage.

One summer morning when the baby was about three months old, Ray came with an offer which determined if i was still to stay with them or not. He told me to nurse their baby while they were at work, I had to be their baby-sitter. It startled me..! *How outrageously impersonal, how cruel his words were!* My heart sank. Ray was not even ashamed of his beast heart. He really wished to make me into his home helper. I cried bitterly but it never helped. He threatened to throw me out of the house if i did not want to be their helper. If only i had somewhere to go, i would have gone. I succumbed to his insinuations and complied to his call.

I cursed the day i was born. I wished my parents were alive to witness the incomprehensible pain i was in. The only uncle i had, had left the village for a mining town to seek for employment.

Time flew, Sam grew into a big boy. We had a special bond. He became my friend, his smile cheered me and i took good care of him. This did not go well with Sue. She convinced her husband, my husband into believing that i was manipulating and bewitching her son. I did not care about her madness and i let her be.

2015 was my fifth year with Ray. I was now tired of everything. Nothing worked between us and i yearned for relief from that situation. One day i took Sam on my back and walked down to the stream just to refresh from the toxic atmosphere at home. Ray and Sue usually got us out of the house while they were on their book marking thing.

Upon reaching the stream, Sam and i sat by the stream bank and we got busy with building sand castles. Suddenly a stranger appeared from our opposite. We took no notice of him, we paid no attention although he tried so hard to attract our attention. He asked for a little time to talk to me. Then he said things that puzzled my head. *Who was he and how did he know all about me.* We had never seen each other before but then he rightly narrated my ordeal just like how Jesus did to the Samaritan woman at a well. I had nothing else to argue with him except to comply with his advice.

When i got home i asked Ray if he could allow me to visit my uncle in the city. Without any hesitation he allowed it as if he was waiting for that moment when i would vacate his premise. It never bothered me; all i wanted was to go to the city for reasons best known to me then. The next morning i left for the city and i said goodbye to everything that haunted my life. The gods had remembered me.

Things went as planned. I started attending lessons at brother Tim's academic college. I worked so hard and i was so much inspired by other classic young women of substance who frequented brother Tim's offices. I re-directed all my energies from being wistful and regretful over a failed marriage into developing myself. Brother Tim became my treasure chest of wisdom. He guided me and i adapted those valuable lessons to my own life.

Brother Tim, as i affectionately called him, became very cheerful to me, he was fun, he was of high intelligence and i highly esteemed him. His words of wisdom always left me awestruck. He wanted the best out of me. He encouraged me and i never disappointed him. He delighted when i came to confide in him in simple and childlike confidence.

I passed my high school examinations and then enrolled at a Law School. A couple of years down the line i graduated as a lawyer, my life had shaped up. I had added value to myself and i was ready to go into the world and exhibit my potential.

Brother Tim was my savior. I learnt on how he made it in life. He told me of his humble beginnings and how he had climbed the ladder of success. He is one of the world's renowned literal artists having gained international acclaim as the *Lord of controversy*, and an important figure who sharpens the writing skills in young budding writers of Africa and beyond.

I lived differently, i was happy. I forgot about Ray and his hideous character. One weekend brother Tim and i decided to pay him a visit and i took with me something important. He was surprised to see the diamond he had trampled on. I served him with divorce papers.

As if it was in a movie, Tim proposed love to me and i felt my tummy churning up and down. *What a happy ending...* Eventually the dust of my past life had turned into a golden haze!

Dear other mommy,
Mimi Machakaire

It hasn't been that long since we last said our goodbyes but I imagine you are up in heaven, settling in very nicely with the other angels. I imagine you gossiping, sharing stories about us and from your time on earth. I imagine so many things for you. This is what brings a smile on my face, knowing that you are in your favorite place. You used to talk about heaven a lot while you were fighting for your life. You said you saw singing birds, green grass and your father late at night. You said you lived in another world that was quite unlike the one you knew but you never feared knowing what was waiting for you. I'll remember you fondly from now on, how we used to talk for hours on end, how you were more than just my aunty but my dearest friend.

How you would always say to call you mommy instead and shop till your heart's content. You traveled and saw the world as beautiful as it is, you would always say how I was your favorite kid. You knew I had my mother and that was fine with you but you would rather be called mommy number two. My fondest memory is the time you came to visit me in a town far from home, you had to make sure that I knew I wasn't alone. We would hop from one restaurant to the other, until you found the wines you liked but I was never bothered because I saw your face in pure delight. I saw myself in a dream last night talking to my mother, thinking an angel tried to visit me and we already knew who it could be.

I think about you a lot dear other mommy, please don't think I've forgotten, just know that I feel sorry. I feel sorry that you suffered an illness for the longest time. I feel sorry that you cried as you were in pain and I couldn't be there to help keep you sane. They always say that this thing called grieving takes time. They always try to tell me how

I feel but those feelings are not mine. They did not know you, they did not know the kind of life you had. They do not know the stories we shared or how much you cared. They do not know everything we've been through but how could they know, for there can only be one you. In this world full of sorrow and uncertainty, I sincerely hope that you are happy. We go day by day wishing you were still here and that things had turned out differently. Despite all that's changed, we still pray for love and serenity. One thing though that I am grateful for, is all the memories that I cherish deep inside of me. My soul is thankful that I got to meet you and get to know you as more than what meets the eye. Little did I know our last picture, would be your way of telling me goodbye.

We might have said our goodbye's while you were still alive but more than anything I wanted you to survive. Dear other mommy, you could see how much I've grown, you saw me happy in your dreams and wanted for death to be postponed. Despite all that you've endured, in your lifetime, you lived a life so freely and more so unapologetically. You lived a life unlike any other, you lived a life like a true mother.

There might have been some things one would say you missed out on, you never got to see your other grandbaby while the world was crying of omicron. You had a birthday right before you died, but you spent it in bed of which knowing all of this still makes me cry. There was a lot of things we had planned and I still hope that I'll wake up one day and this will all be a bad dream just like Alice had in wonderland. While they say I might be in this denial phase, I have come to accept that we can still talk in other ways.

I know that you can hear me when I pray, thank you for the lessons and the stories, I'll never forget your ways. Until we meet again, my dearest other mommy. Please remember that, I'll love you forever and for always. I'll see you once more, and we will go back to the way things used to be but I hope for now you're watching over me and the rest of our family.

Dear other mommy, your very character is engraved in all of my memories. I still have gifts and pictures you left with me. Every time I hear a bird singing, I will think of you. I will think of how you made your heavenly debut. It was a very hard birthday for me this year. You died the same week I was born and for this left me in tears. Someone said not to worry because you would have wanted to see me happy. This we choose to celebrate your life, of which I thought it the best advice. The only thing that I wanted to do to spend the day was a picnic on a weakened getaway. My fear was knowing there was a high chance it may rain and for this I prayed. I prayed it wouldn't rain on my special day and sure enough things actually went my way.

I could have sworn that it was you, advocating for me up there. I could feel your presence with me in the air. I like the idea that there's an angel I know personally, there's an angel in heaven fighting for me. There's an angel looking after our family and more importantly, there's an angel who is my other mommy. In all my life I've never had a death that's hit as close to my heart as this. It makes me imagine my soul one day, disappearing into some abyss. It makes me wonder, what happens before we arrive to the other side. I remember you tried to tell me before you died. You were in a deep long sleep and came back to tell the tale. You never saw much of what they said you would but then you said you tried to help those you could. You said some were lost and you were there to help them find their way, I can't help but wonder if you were helped on the day.

Did you walk your way into the heavenly light? Or did someone escort you to where you were supposed to be? I have so many questions what did you see? Sometimes I wish you could pay me a visit as you are, considering you are not that far. Sometimes I wish you could give me a hint on who I should trust. Sometimes I wish you could warn me on who I should leave in the dust. Sometimes I wish you could tell me what the future holds. Sometimes I wish you could be oh so bold and tell me if everything they said was true or if everything is what we already knew. My heart is aching every day for you. I feel sad, mad, and guilty and numb all at once but all in all, yes I still feel your presence. Even though it may not be physical, or digital or anything that I can see, in my heart, you will always be.

Dearest other mommy, as I write this letter it makes me feel better, knowing after all this time, I can still call you mine. I can still connect with you in other ways, I can still hear your voice in each and every prayer.

As I grow older in these 27 years of life, you once told me how happy you were to hear that one day, I will be someone's wife. While we are all still grieving and missing you, I hope that you will still attend my wedding because you will have the greatest view. I still have conversations we had, stored within my phone and the last text you sent me was asking when will I be giving you all grandbabies. It made me smile and laugh, thinking despite how sick you were it was something on your mind. I told you not to worry for all will happen in its own time. With all that's said and done, to be honest we were given all the warning signs. We were told that one day you may not be here but we were still not ready and hoped we'd get at least one more year.

You fought so hard and you were scared that you were letting us down but you are still queen in our eyes and you possess one of the biggest crowns. We have a special bond, this I know no one can break. I also know that I'll save you a piece of our wedding cake. I visited you as often as I could while you were still alive, we met for different events but the love you gave me was truly heaven sent. There will be no one quite like you, this I know to be true. Thank you for it all, thank you for being you. Thank you for the kids you created, who have become my friends. Thank you for fighting until the very end. If there's one thing I know for sure, it is that the next time when I see you in my dreams, I'll know exactly what it means.

Love always,

Your favorite daughter

Mimi

P.S. *The world will know your story one day. The story of how we came to be. The story of aunty Euna, my other mommy.*

THE AFRICAN SPIRITS SPEAK

Jabulani Mzinyathi

[commenced 19.05.2020]

INTRODUCTION

Over the years I have been thinking about what it means to be an African. What really does it mean to be African? Some say we are just from the land of Cush. Others say we are from Ethiopia and that the whole of what we now call Africa was then called Ethiopia. This work is a collection of those thoughts. They have been expressed in poetry and prose form. These works are akin to a street fight. They have no definite form. In a street fight anything goes. These works are a response to the effects of slavery, colonialism, neo-colonialism and recolonisation. The carving of Africa into Anglophone, Lusophone, Francophone… Africa is still a major draw back to African unity. Africans view each other as foreigners whereas until recently Europe was dismantling its boundaries and using a common currency and easing trade within Europe. This will touch on a number of issues that affect African development. I call upon African spirits to speak through me. I choose to be possessed by those warrior spirits so that generations to come may take the baton and liberate Africa. The struggle continues. Even as I write this I still have questions at the back of my mind. It is my fervent hope that translators will have work on their hands and have this work in many African languages. It is a very real possibility.

Emancipate yourselves from mental slavery

172

The subtitle is made up of the words of the Jamaican reggae poet, prophet, philosophy, singer, song writer- Robert Nesta Marley. He remains an unapologetic pan African. I write of him in the present for he lives in spirit inspiring generations. His timeless lyrics still inspire hope to many in Africa and beyond.

Emancipation from mental slavery is a chilling reminder of the fact that the oppressor dwells now in the mind of the not so conscious oppressed. The shackles and chains were removed when slavery was abolished but the oppressor remains happily ensconced in the mind of the oppressed. When reference is made to slavery this must be seen in the context of colonialism, neo-colonialism and re-colonization at the hands of many world powers with China taking a wicked lead.

The oppressor lives in the mind

The most powerful oppressor is the one who lives in the mind of the oppressed. That is the essence of psychological warfare. The oppressed is made to feel worthless. It is drummed into the mind that you are worth nothing. You are made to believe that the oppressor is a god to be worshipped and that without the oppressor then nothing moves. Self doubt is firmly entrenched in the mind of the oppressed. Against this background Marcus Garvey states that without confidence one is defeated in the race of life before they have even started but with confidence they have won before they have even started.

My purpose has not been to romanticize the African past but to make fellow Africans realize that the sky is not even the limit. I draw from the warrior spirits that have fought for African emancipation. That is the well I drink from. The same well that Peter Tosh drank from. He sings of the fight that he will put up till Africa and Africans are free. That is the fight I am in.

The African spirits speak now. There is urgent need to forge real men and women between the hammer and tongs of repression. The African was never created to be a hewer of wood and drawer of water. Time to get out of this morass is at hand. The earlier we wage a war against the self denigration the better for the Africa and African we want.

Many a time I have spoken about the fact that if one wants to dominate another person you seek to belittle them and destroy their self esteem. One of the phenomenon to use is the language used to describe someone. In the Zimbabwean set up this was done by never recognizing a black man as a man. He was a perpetual minor hence a boy forever. So if one delivered letters, tended gardens, brewed tea he was a post boy, garden boy and tea boy respectively. There was yet another boy who was a snitch employed to lord it over fellow sufferers. That was the baas' boy. That means a boss's boy. This one had a false consciousness. He became more oppressive than the colonizer or oppressor.

Where the perpetual boy lived was the boy's kaya. The word khaya means home in isiNdebele. Boy's kaya means the home where the boy lives. The boy would doff his hat before the boss and the pikinini boss- the oppressor's child who was much younger than the boy.

I will not dwell much on what was. I move on to what is. It seems to me that there was no common goal in the war of liberation. It seems there were competing interests between those that sought total emancipation and those that were bent on taking the place of the erstwhile oppressor. These I call the apes. These are the people that have continued to call their employees garden boys especially after they moved to the leafy suburbs. Perhaps they do not realize the impact of the language use or they have the oppressor ensconced in their minds and see themselves as being better than their fellow sufferers.

I have said it that I ask that the African spirits be here with me as I go through this soul searching work. The spirits of Walter Rodney, Haile Selassie, Kwame Nkrumah, Patrice Lumumba, Thomas Sankara and many more are humbly asked to be here and see that this work reaches to the many parched minds out there. The chasms among our people are so deep rooted that we have urgent need to critically look at who we are as a nation. We have common socio-economic-political links that we have been blinded to. The divide and rule tactics used against us continue to this day. In the name of international law we have been taught to treat as sacrosanct the colonial boundaries that have been our worst enemy. We cling to small territories that in some cases may not be economically viable as countries in their own right. We are seen as lesser beings that cannot have a single entity in the form of the United States of Africa. They are able in America to have the United States of Africa. We have had that dream but our worst enemy is power hunger and clinging onto western perceptions of sovereignty.

African spirituality

In many parts of Africa today people are so engrossed in the Christian faith but have perhaps forgotten that this religion was by way of imposition and was even resisted by our forebears. People had to be converted to Christianity by missionaries. I am not writing about that process in any indepth way but just stating a raw fact. The missionaries came and preached about a new God and talked about the father, the son and the holy ghost. I do not know how the ghost can ever be holy. As I write this I am keenly aware that this will be described as heresy. Frankly I do not care a hoot about that. Posterity must make informed choices.

The Christian missionaries came to Africa and talked about Jesus Christ. That was in keeping with their faith. To demonstrate that our people dabbled in apostasy they began to talk about Jesu Kristu. One can detect an attempt to fit in. The worshipping of Mwari in Chishona and Unkulunkulu in IsiNdebele was labelled ancestral worship and therefore pagan. That is the thinking to this day. When I meet people and they ask which church I go to and I say none they look at me like I am an alien just landed from space. That I link with my living dead and pray to God through my ancestors is deemed evil and pagan and they pray that I may see the light, a damascene moment and join them in their alien and adopted ways.

My view is that the African knew of the existence of a superior being called musiki/umdali meaning creator. I will find out other words used in other languages. For now it is about my identity as confined to the area between the Limpopo to the south and the Zambezi to the north, the eastern highlands and the western border with Botswana. I must reiterate that these borders are an imposition that are the aftermath of the 1884 Berlin conference. We have clung to these in keeping with international law principles. Whose international law principles?

The rise of Islam in Africa will be attended to here and now. There are fights in several African countries. There are some bent on establishing

Islamic states in Africa. I wonder how Africans fit in the Islamic scheme of things. To me this is another form of veering off the African spirituality. Both Christianity and Islam point towards apostasy. It is about time Africans turn to their ancestors' ways. Without that they will always be spiritual emptiness and also they will not prosper in other spheres of life. A person's spirituality impacts on even their economic production. That explains what I have seen with the Pakistanis and how they close shop to go and do their prayers. One can never tempt them to go on working during their lunch break. They simply go to their mosques and pray.

In order to draw us away from what I will call African traditional religion, our ways have been termed ancestral worship. The truth of the matter is that we do not worship our ancestors. We have our ancestors as intercessors. This thinking is denigrated by trying to bring into the equation scientific principles in issues metaphysical. There is no way these issues can be put in a test tube and scientifically proved as happens in the natural sciences. There is no way the birth of Jesus Christ can be proved scientifically. The birth of a child to a virgin is unheard of in the natural sciences.

Raising African consciousness through poetry

The poems that make up this part of the work are written in order to make the present and the future sit up and do serious introspection about which way to go. For now Africa is largely ruled by a caretaker class of rulers doing so on behalf of Europe, America and China largely. What we have is flag and national anthem independence. The fragmented economies of Africa are not in the hands of the majority. The African continent sells its resources for a song and buys finished

177

goods at exorbitant prices. One wonders why there is no value addition? One wonders why jobs are being exported in a continent where there is mass unemployment especially among the youths. The youths are now drowning in alcohol and mind bending drugs instead of being economically productive. Speak African spirits. The future must hear what you have to say. As Peter Tosh says in Not Gonna Give It Up : Africa is the richest place but now is home to the poorest race and to me it's just a disgrace. He goes on to say we got to fight cause it's not wrong. The time demands turning ploughshares into swords. The fight is a righteous fight.

Arise afrika arise

Siphoning our raw materials still
While in abject poverty we wallow
Taking away our gold, diamonds, platinum
While our bodies we adorn with fake jewellery

Propagating their Anglophone ideas
Spreading their francophone thinking
Somewhere lusophone ideas held supreme
African philosophies on the dung heap

The poisoned and stunted present crop
Choosing to forget Marcus Mosiah Garvey
Choosing to forget Kwame Nkrumah
Choosing to remove reggae from the airwaves

That dream should now bear fruit
These chasms have to be bridged

The senseless bickering should now end
Africa with mud and spittle get your sight

Afrika Day Reflections

The bandits came from lands far away
Came from across seas and oceans
Came armed with the maxim gun
Came armed with a warped interpretation
A weird, warped interpretation of the bible
Came to redeem the pagan from himself
The uncivilized with their brand of civilization
All they did was to satisfy their lust
Raped her and she bear the scars still
The mental and physical scars there still
The raw wounds there to this day

She still is a victim of rape today
Repeatedly raped by kith and kin now
Raped by mercenaries masquerading as liberators
Her children wail with no end in sight
Her children washed away by rivers of squalor
Her children yearning for the sun to shine again
Her children locked in combat with bandits
Those from home and from lands far away

Taking Off The Yoke

Slave driver
Avarice you taught my people
Self denigration
You drummed into them
Colonial boundaries now they observe
Afrika you labeled-dark continent
Our ways you called pagan
Our civilization you termed backward
Your backwardness you termed progress
Divisions- the seed you sowed

See my resilience lives
See your pagan ways crumble
See the abundance of my pride
For your wickedness you shall pay
No more shall we be slaves
Our ancestors fight with renewed vigour
Slave driver, your time is up

United States of Afrika

In this blood
That dream lives
Bridging the chasms
Shattering their nightmares
That dream lives

The Cape to Cairo dream
Not that bandit's evil dream
Marcus Mosiah Garvey
Kwame Nkrumah…
That dream lives in this blood

Those evil schemes see
Anglophone Afrika
Francophone afrika
Lusophone Afrika
What a farce
Afrika transcend these barriers

My Share

Just a piece of pure gold
Just a piece of an uncut diamond
What about a piece of platinum
That son of Africa in the diaspora
Wailing in that song of revolution
'Africa is the richest place
But now is home to the poorest race'
Impoverished by gluttonous Europe
Leaving us fighting over the crumbs
Leaving us with holes in the ground
See the big fight behind this humility

Civilization

I am invoking the spirits of Afrika to the best of my abilities. I am asking fellow citizens of the United States of Afrika to make this ideal work. The road is long, winding, foggy and blistering. Freedom cannot be given on a silver platter. There will be blood, sweat and tears.

I am aware of the iron smelting that had long started at Great Dzimbahwe. The empirical evidence is there. The making of tools from iron had long begun. Our people had long started the use of the crude form of the blast furnace. That development train was derailed. Even with empirical evidence self doubt has been implanted in most minds.

Evidence of mathematics and architecture at Great Zimbabwe has been attributed to the Arabs. All this is an attempt to show that the African had to be civilized by a gun and bible wielding Caucasian. There is no explanation about penetration into Dlodlo and Nalatale. I am not sure how they explain away the same structures at Mapungubwe in what is now known as South Africa.

The stone structures that remain sturdy today with no cement have baffled our detractors and they refuse to attribute their construction to great Afrikan men and women of the time. The entrance to the Great enclosure where a single pillar sustains a high wall baffles them. They want our children to doubt that a black man could have constructed that.

We are informed that the colonizer brought civilization and we could have been living in caves. They conveniently forget their own story of living in caves and animal skins too. The sad part is the Afrikan who believes that the black man was taming his environment to suit his own purposes. The story that is told is one of stagnation.

I have always asked myself lots of questions about this concept of civilization. Where is the civilization of one who comes into the home of another and snatches women, men and children, load them on slave ships? Where is the civilization of one who then throws over board bodies of those that die on the way and does not even accord them a decent burial? Where is the civilization of one who uproots fellow human beings from their natural environment and ships them as slaves across the oceans in shackles and chains? Where is the civilization of one who comes armed with guns to forcibly move Africans from their land and then sit down in Berlin and plan fragmentation of African communities. They cannot stand on moral high ground and claim to have civilized us.

Afrika Day

Every year on 25 May Afrika Day is celebrated. I am not so sure if there are any real celebrations that go on in Afrika. I have over the years written poems that show that Afrika is yet to celebrate. This year I will celebrate by way of a poem in honour of Ambassador Arikana Chihombori Quao. My view which I have already seen being hotly contested is that her is an African woman who is singing the right song. She is a spiritual backing vocalist for Peter Tosh and other singers who sang about Africa.

Here is what Peter Tosh says in the song Not Gonna Give It Up:

Africans don't wait too long

We gotta fight cause it's not wrong
Won't join me and sing this song

He goes on to say:

Afrika is the richest place
But is home to the poorest race
And to me it's just a disgrace.

This is the song that Ambassador Chihombori has been singing. She has said Afrikans should unite, those at home and those abroad. She has exposed the evil umbilical cord tying Afrika to the colonizers. They cannot be erstwhile colonizers because the shackles and chains are still around. The independence in most Afrikan States is flag, national anthem and change of name of country independence.

Afrika is still the exporter of raw materials and importer of finished goods at exorbitant prices. As already stated Afrika exports jobs when its young generation is on the streets with diplomas and degrees but no job. Many lives are in ruins due to frustration wrought by unemployment. Many youths have turned to drugs in a bid to avert stress. They do not realize that they are adding petrol to a burning fire.

There are lots of questions that arise as to what is being celebrated in Afrika each year. There are lots of gluttonous leaders on the continent. They have fat bank accounts in Swiss banks. They also have mansions in Dubai, Singapore, Malaysia and other places. They do not build schools at home so they take their children to study abroad. They do not build hospitals. They do not maintain even what they inherited from the colonizers so they fly to China, Singapore and other places to seek medical attention.

So when they meet and celebrate Afrika Day one wonders what is being celebrated? The Afrikan Union is just ineffectual. Dictators do not get a spanking. Human rights abuses galore and this goes on unabated with the AU hardly taking any meaningful action. Elections are a farce as they are rigged in most cases. The AU endorses some of these scandals as being free and fair. It is a shame.

Aesthetics

The extent of alienation is deeply entrenched. I am happy though that some people have stood up and challenged Eurocentric perceptions of what constitutes a beautiful woman. I have always been against what I see at beauty pageants. The pencil thin and self starving young woman is rewarded as an epitome of beauty. I am not against any woman who is naturally not big. What I loathe is this business of getting to a point of near starvation in order to wear the so called crown of beauty at these beauty pageants.

The African spirits in me have described a beautiful woman as having a wholesome bust. Added to it is an enticingly big behind. The Sarah/ Saartjie Baartman type. They even took her to Europe to look at her natural endowments in sadistic fashion. They dehumanized her. To me she is an epitome of a beautiful Afrikan woman not a symbol of sexual primitiveness.

Colonial perceptions of beauty still persist. Many of our dark, beautiful woman erase their beauty by applying dangerous substances to their

185

faces. They have been taught that to be beautiful is to be light skinned. That is furthest from the truth. They are exposing themselves to skin cancers. They have for long been protect from such by their melanin- a natural endowment. It is sad that they do not notice that white women come to Africa and are happy to do sun tanning.

There is also this stupid thing they do to their hair. They cover that up with all kinds from other parts of the world. It gives them a lot of discomfort as they repeatedly scratch their dandruff or even lice infested scalps.

The revolution cannot be complete when the mind is not rid of such self denigration.

There is a trend where our mbira music is not appreciated by our own people. Dumi Maraire, Stella Chiweshe and many others like Tafadzwa Matamba draw crowds among no Africans. People in foreign lands are appreciating our music. Our people have no time for that. My view is that we have been brought up on western tastes. Many schools would have clubs where children were taught ball room dancing. There was very little or no lessons in traditional dances like mhande, isitshikitsha, muchongoyo and other African traditional dances. There are many in Europe now learning to play the mbira and yet this has been shunned by our people largely. It is sad indeed.

Traditional medicines

A few years ago I was diagnosed to be diabetic by one Dr Tendai Chimbganda. She is in fact my doctor and friend. I long left marondera where I was a magistrate. I have since left magistracy and now am a lawyer in beitbridge. A digression there for you.

Following the advice of Dr Chimbganda I made a lot of dietary changes. This was to lower the blood sugar levels that were shockingly high. When I walked into her surgery she was shocked. She wondered why I was still on my feet when I should be in a coma. The reading was thirty-three milligrams per one hundred milligrams.

She lectured my wife and I on the food I was to consume. She also put me on a metformin regime. She said I was to take this for life.

I was devastated. I however vowed to fight it. Through the late one Mashoko Ndengu I had met one soft spoken Mr Tudu an ex body guard of the late Robert Mugabe. Mr Tudu gave me some herbs to deal with the diabetes problem.

The sugar levels dropped. These have been normal for a long time. I test using my glucometer. I have now given up on metformin. I am into herbal mixtures. I have been informed that there are unpleasant side effects of these western medicines.

I have made a vow to resort to traditional medicines in dealing with ailments. The African spirits speak. It is time to go back home. Go back there to the warm hearth of our home. The revolution has in earnest commenced. There is no going back into slave mode.

I have explained before that traditional medicines have been derisively labelled mishonga yechibhoyi. Chibhoyi means that which belongs to a boy. I have previously explained that using that term is self denigration of the highest order. The African man was never a man. He was always a boy hence boy's kaya, tea boy, garden boy, baas boy etc. so I am back to mishonga yechivanhu. That means traditional medicines to the uninitiated.

Language

As I write this work I grapple with the question of language. I always ask myself why I should write this in English. I ask why I should not use chiShona which is my mother tongue. I also enjoy the work done by Chenjerai Hove in Bones and also Gabriel Okara's The Voice. They have come up with a certain way of expressing themselves in some kind of English that takes into account local idioms, that is idioms peculiar to their local settings.

This work to some extent is in the same mould with Decolonising The Mind by Ngugi Wa Thiong'o. The language debate will be here for a long time. That is healthy. The question of the target audience will also be here for a long time. I however have no qualms with anyone writing in any language. There will always be room for translations. So these ideas must be propagated through translations.

There have been suggestions that kiSwahili must be adopted as the language for Africa. Let the debates continue. This can only be healthy. I have been a participant in debates or discussions about language.

I have been exposed to some Kinyarwanda and Luhya words. I found a lot in common with my mother tongue chiShona. There is a lot that we have in common as Africans. We should be taking time to find each other in this tower of Babel. The lusophone, Anglophone, francophone crap must never be reason for us to remain divided. The following words illustrate what I am trying to get at:

188

Umuriro kumulilo umlilo fire
Inkoko ingokho inkukhu huku fowl
Inzu indlu house
Imbeba mbeva mouse
Ingwe leopard
Urugendo luchendo rwendo gwendo journey
Inzara nzara hunger

These words are from the languages chiShona, Kinyarwanda, Luhya
and one or two from isiNdebele. One needs not be a rock scientist to
note that there are similarities.

Questions, hope and determination in Nomzamo Dube's Milk, Bile and Honey
Review by Nkosiyazi Kan Kanjiri

The genesis of the Zimbabwean diaspora which has become more pronounced in recent years can be traced back to as early as 1980, when then it was perceived to be paranoid White Rhodesians leaving the country for fear of persecution from black administration. This was despite the reconciliation mood of the time. Paranoia from white Rhodesians made sense then in the face of an overwhelmingly black majority government. But how does one explain the flight of fellow black Zimbabweans who left the country a few years after independence when the country still prided itself as the breadbasket of Africa?

Surely, in a country with a vibrant economy coupled with the independence euphoria of the time, one is expected to sing "there is no place like home". But what happens when that song becomes nothing but just a cliché? Poetry lovers would tell you it is at moments like these that the only convincing explanation comes from poets like Warsan Shire. In the poem Home, Warsan Shire writes, "No one leaves home until home is a sweaty voice in your ear saying- leave, run away from me now, I don't know what I have become but I know that anywhere is safer than here". Milk, Bile and Honey is the story of a man who hears the whisper in Warsan Shire's poem, Home and obeys.

When the war ends, Nomzamo Dube's protagonist becomes a fugitive and begins a war of destiny. A simultaneous war that involves running away from the freedom he fought for on one hand, and facing his unresolved past on the other. He is still that man born out of wedlock, now on a quest to know his father. But there is another thing, he makes a girl pregnant and denies responsibility.

There is a lot that happens in a country learning how to be free. Equally, there is a lot that happens to a boy turned into a man by the war and now has to learn to be a father by himself. These are the circumstances that shape the protagonist's character in Nomzamo Dube's debut novel, Milk, Bile and Honey.

The issues explored are gripping, but how the story begins is even more compelling, "How could a mother carry a child for 9 months and not in the process think about a list of names to pick from?" Anyone who has ever attempted to write a book will confess writing is no child's play and what is even more difficult is how to begin the story.

I have read three books whose beginning, like Milk Bile and Honey is absorbing. Tsitsi Dangarembwa begins her award-winning novel Nervous Conditions in a seemingly insensitive yet captivating way "I was not sorry when my brother died." Petina Gappah's Book of Memory begins in a rather simplistic yet sophisticated manner, "The story that you have asked me to tell you does not begin with the pitiful ugliness of Lloyd's death." Those who have read Dambudzo Marechera will not forget the, "I got my things and left" line that begins his novella, House of Hunger. Milk Bile and Honey begins with an effortless question, one that seeks answers.

Written in first person narration and spiced with humor, Nomzamo Dube makes you fall in love, empathize and more importantly adopt the protagonist's inquisitive personality which is evident at the beginning of the story. Reading the book, you cannot help but ask, "How can a man who knows the pain of growing without a father deny impregnating the girl he loves?" or "How can a man fight for freedom then runs away from it?" But as highlighted earlier, there is a lot that happens to a man learning to be a father in a country learning how to be free. One of the many things is captured in Joshua Nkomo's book,

The Story of My Life when he says "a nation can win freedom without its people becoming free"

The protagonist is a relatable character. He is a patriotic citizen repelled by his own country. He leaves for South Africa, leaving behind a beautiful girl pregnant with his child. Life in the diaspora is not easy as an undocumented immigrant .The circumstances he finds himself in are the same circumstances many Zimbabweans, young and old, find themselves in now. However, Nomzamo Dube does not see her story as connecting with the larger Zimbabwean story.

"I was just writing a story, oblivious of the issues and lessons thereof. This book is based on a true story and I felt compelled to document the life of someone I know, someone I regard close to me". This is the response I got from Nomzamo Dube when I engaged her after reading her book. For a story like Milk, Bile and Honey, this is too simple a response, honestly. One would have thought the author was aware that her story, though just a story, as she puts it, is a story that goes beyond the horizons of her own imaginations and the realities that shape her main character.

Milk, Bile and Honey is not just about Nomzamo Dube's protagonist. To regard it as such, even as the author sees it as such would be a selfish act. The story is about many Zimbabweans and everyone who identifies with the protagonist.

The book is a multi-themed story. It touches, in the larger scheme of things, issues of tribalism and failed nation building. It also summons a revisiting and questioning of history in terms of the Zimbabwe's liberation struggle. In a more particular sense, it explores family politics in a patriarchal society, love and marriage, religion and its relief effect. But above all, the story is about individual determination and hope.

Milk, Bile and Honey is a story of solemnity garnished with humor. It flows with the complexity of a male story told from a feminine point of view. In her own words Nomzamo Dube says, "Writing the story made me understand the world of men and how it shapes their behavior towards women".

Zimbabweans in Germany: the Isusu Ffena Festival
Interview by Tanaka Chidora
Photography by Dico Baskoro

In 2022, from 12 –13 August, I was one of the headlining talents at the Isusu Ffena Festival in Berlin. I read poems from my collection, *Because Sadness is Beautiful?* (2019) and held an exciting conversation with the moderator, Mareika, and the audience. The session also featured Tanatsei Gambura who read from her collection, *Things I Have Forgotten Before* (2021). A couple of months later, I (TC) set up a meeting with Mareika Chirikure (**MC**) to talk about Isusu Ffena and the work the collective is doing in Germany.

TC: Basically, what I'm doing is that I'm working with my publisher who publishes a volume of poetry every year called *Zimbolicious*. I think the first volume was published a pre-2010 and it actually became one of the most popular and heavily subscribed creative arts anthologies in Zimbabwe. So, he is trying to continue that legacy of publishing new and established voices in Zimbabwe's literary scene, and conversations concerning the literary arts. Of course, he's also expanded to involve other forms of art like sculpture and the like, but principally, it's about poetry. So, this year I am the guest editor and as a guest editor I was given the priviledge to bring a feature of my choice. To tell you the truth, I really liked the Isusu Ffena Festival in Berlin. Besides the fact that I was reading my poetry, I think you guys are doing a great thing. So, I decided to do a feature called 'Zimbabweans in Germany' and how Zimbabweans interact in the arts sector in Germany, specifically focusing on what Isusu Ffena is doing to unite Zimbabweans in Germany and Europe using arts festivals. Before proceeding, I want to congratulate you for holding the Isusu Ffena festival this year. It was an amazing experience for me.

MC: Thank you, Tanaka. I also want to thank you for joining us. To tell you the truth, people are still talking about you and telling us how you entertained them with your poetry and the conversations we had. We received very good feedabck, so we thank you for that.

TC: I really appreciate, thank you. So, tell us, when did Isusu Ffena start?

MC: Isusu Ffena started off as another project called the Isusu Festival, and Nora, my sister, who was part of the collective, co-organised the Isusu Festival in 2019. I supported her, of course, but not in an active sense. I attended the festival, but Nora is the one who organised it. That was when she realized that it was quite a burden to organise a festival by yourself and to organise all of those things by yourself, especially where there is a good reception. She wanted to continue doing it, so she reached out to a few people who she thought might be of interest to work with, and to kind of build something up; so, that's how we created that idea of Isusu Ffena. It is different from Isusu Festival in many ways. The Isusu Ffena Festival is a collective of five people and four of us are from Zimbabwe (Isusu meaning 'us' in Shona), and the fifth is from Uganda (Ffena meaning 'together' in Luganda). We did our first festival in 2020 and we had a great time regardless of the advent of Covid-19 and attendant restrictions, and also regardless of the fact that it was our first festival. In 2021 the restrictions in Germany were much tighter, so we weren't able to do the festival. What we tried was to do a lot of online events, like hosting people and having different discussions with people online. And now, we are in our third year, and we've had our second festival, which is the one you participated in. Usually our festivals follow a theme and, as you know, our theme for 2022 was *Community and Identities in a New Cityscape*. For our first festival in 2020 the theme focused on Germany's colonial history, especially the Berlin Conference. So we were kind of exploring what that means for people who are coming from African

195

countries and are now living in Europe, especially Germany. We were also looking at how Germany is thinking about her colonial history. That's just a brief overview of what we're doing as Isusu Ffena.

Tanaka reading some of his poems fron Because Sadness is Beautiful?

TC: Awesome! So, is there any kind of love collaboration with any organisation in Germany or Germany itself?

MC: We have collaborated with a lot of different groups, in the sense of getting funding for the festival, volunteers and space. Also, to be able to afford to have artists coming in and all of these things, we need a budget. So we have been collaborating with different organizations, like the space in which we held the festival, Callie's, for instance. We have also worked with other groups that are already doing something similar. For example, in terms of exploring the colonial history in Germany we have worked with EOTO (i don't know if you know them) which is a group of black German people. They have a space, a library, and work on bringing black people in Germany together. They have done extensive work on exploring the history of black people in Germany, German colonial history and the like. So they are really strong a partner for us. In all of our events, say a panel discussion, a workshop or a festival, we partner with different people, different artists. What we try to do is that we make it a collaborative experience between Isusu Ffena and whoever we are working with. People can also bring in their inputs and things like that, because we're trying to create an environment where we can exchange ideas. So it's not just about us coming in and saying this is what we want to do. If we want to work with a specific artist, for example, we can think about what that artist wants to do with us, collaboratively speaking. A good example is Medine who has been exhibiting with Isusu Ffena since we started. Whenever we deal with Medine, we always do it as a collaborative experience. She looks at our theme and kind of takes it and creates something on her own, and if she needs assistance, for example with models and spaces for taking the pictures, we provide those. So yeah, we are just trying to have a kind collaboration where we bring with an artist who in turn creates something based on our theme, something that's good for us and for the artists as well.

TC: I have seen Medine's work. I think she is quite well-known in terms of the extensive exhibitions she has held around the world. How have you managed to convince her? Also, where is she originally from? I know I am asking a cliched question here.

MC: Medine's cultural heritage is a combination of many countries. Her parents are from Ivory Coast, she was born and raised in France and lives in Berlin. How did we meet her? When you are in the Berlin arts scene, you meet a lot of people. That's how we came across her work. She is somebody who is not just an artist we are working with, but someone we can consider a friend. In the first year of our festival, Norah had a concept that she wanted to do, and she approached Medine and asked her if she wanted to contribute to the concept. We managed to convince her to work with us because Isusu Ffena is a conducive environment for her in the sense that it allows her to create these exhibitions which she can go on to show in other places. Medine has so far created three original exhibitions for us and she has taken these exhibitions to other places. So it's not only a matter of taking existing pictures and exhibiting them; Isusu Ffena is a platform for the creation of new concepts, a springboard for her to be able to create new content. We have also received help with some funding to help with the printing of the pictures, the framing and provision of the models. So it's been a collaborative experience where she also gets something out of it. That's what we try to do with all our artists, for example, with you, we also tried to like sell your books at the festival so that people get to know about your work. So, while we're really interested in having a good and exciting festival, we are also interested in creating strong relationships with people and giving them the feeling that oh, you know, I feel like my work is being valued; maybe I can do more with it. In terms of our budget (which is quite low if you compare it with other big festivals that have been hosted in Berlin), we can't convince people through funding, so we need to convince people in other ways.

Nora outlinig the objectives of the festival

TC: Judging from my experience at the 2022 festival, there was this feeling of community that animated the festival. Would you say the festival is the go-to place for Africans in Berlin and in Germany in general?

MC: I don't think it is that yet, but I do think that we're getting there. There are other big festivals and African festivals that are also held in Berlin, but I would like to think that there is something that is unique about Isusu Ffena's setup. I think you've already mentioned that it has that community feeling to it. The whole concept was motivated by the fact that we were living in Berlin while identifying as Africans. We discovered that all the events and places that we went to didn't have us in mind, even as the audience. So you would go to an African festival only to have this feeling that it was more about putting Africans on a stage for Europeans. Therefore, we wanted to create a vibe for our people; we wanted to create a community feeling, where you feel like okay, we can come and we can do these things. I think that's kind of what has made us unique. Also, we build a relationship with the people that we work with to cultivate that community feeling. You can feel that when you get there. But would I say we are the number one place to go to for African artists? I do not think so. But if you give us a couple of years, we will get there. What's encouraging, though, is that in the beginning, we used to look for artists to come and partner us, and that at a time when no one knew about us, so it was really difficult to get artists on board, but now, we have artists getting in touch with us and wanting to partner us. I believe there is value in the things that are doing; we're getting more traction, especially when you artists come to us and want to work with us. This year's festival was encouragingly subscribed. Those two days of the festival were a prelude to what the future of the festival will really look like, and I can say the future is bright.

TC: I have also seen that beyond finding a space for people who identify as Africans, who live in Germany, specifically in Berlin, the festival also attracts people who do not identify as Africans. How have you managed to market the festival beyond just appealing to people who identify as Africans?

MC: This is a very good question actually. I think what you often have in a place like Berlin and in Germany as a whole are diverse people and cultures, so you often have certain groups sticking together, for example Nigerian students' union hold events that cater for their group. In our case, we have worked with different artists who have managed to attract different crowds. You might have noticed, for example, that at this year's festival, the day one crowd was very different from the day two crowd. We have made an active effort to have a range of events to cater for different crowds. Let me briefly talk about our 2020 festival. It was a ten-day event with a range of activities, including panel discusssions (which we didn't really have this year), workshops, exhibitions and so on. When we realised that each event had a unique crowd, we decided to widen the range of our events. This is why we want to work with a range of artists who can bring in different people, different audiences. For example, we know that there are African students in Berlin, and if we want to cater for those we would have afrobeat or amapiano parties. The goal is to appeal to more people. We are also thinking around attracting older people and having events that suit them. We want to make people feel comfortable being at the festival. Our belief is that whoever you are, whatever you identify as, Isusu Ffena is that place where you belong, feel at home and learn. Most importantly, we are a collective that is Pan-African; we want to highlight Pan-African creatives. So we are very much biased towards Africa. I do believe, however, that the reach of African creatives goes beyond Africa. Art's themes have a universal appeal. This explains why we have those diverse crowds.

TC: From the composition of the coordinators of the festival, 4 out of five are from Zimbabwe. How has the reception been like among Zimbabweans in Berlin?

MC: The reception has been very good, I would say, in the sense that as Isusu Ffena, we have been supported immensely by Zimbabweans, not just in Berlin, but outside Berlin. For example, we have Nozi who was one of the volunteers at the festival and who came all the way from Stuttgart, or Chenge who travelled all the way to Berlin to work for us at the festival. Taona the DJ came from Hamburg and helped us to set up the sound system. So there are many things we wouldn't have done without Zimbabweans. But I also feel that part of the reason we have received this support is because members of the Zimbabwean community see a part of themselves in what we do.

TC: I did feel the same way at this year's festival. Besides the fact that I was headlining the festival, I also felt at home. I was part of this diverse crowd of people from all over the world but who were united into a family by Isusu Ffena. But beyond Zimbabweans in Germany, have you also received support from organisations that belong to Zimbabwe like the Zimbabwean Embassy in Berlin?

MC: No, we haven't had support from the Embassy. We have reached out to them to say, this is what we are doing, you know, to kind of let them know what we as Zimbabweans were doing. But we haven't had any official collaboration with the Embassy. I think it's one of three things: on the one hand, you don't know how to approach these topics, like, this is what we want to talk about and we don't know how such things will be perceived. The second is just a matter of the connections that we've had in Germany. I think we haven't had many connections, including with the Embassy. Much of the funding we have received is linked to our own personal and professional lives as members of the collective. While we have sent out invitations to the Embassy, and several African embassies, we have people coming from the embassies as guests in their own private capacity, and not as representatives of the embassies. The funding we have officially received so far was given to us by the African Network of Germany which partially funded our 2020 Festival. They are based primarily in Freiburg but have offices all over Germany. The network has stronger links with African embassies in Germany. I also think that there is this generational gap: picture a scenario where a group of young girls are running a festival; there are chances that elderly people who man these embassies wouldn't take you seriously. But I hope going forward, we will be able to forster a productive relationship with the Zimbabwean and African embassies in Germany.

TC: I think that what you're saying basically reflects even what happens in Zimbabwe itself. There is this tenuous relationship between the arts and the formal institutions in Zimbabwe, including, principally, the State. You will see that most funding, for example, comes from NGOs and rarely from the government. What do you think the future holds in terms of the relationship between artists and govermnmental organisations in Zimbabwe?

MC: I think people want to kind of have their say in many fields of art, especially when working with specific governmental organisations. It's a kind of relationship where governmental organisations expect you to project certain values or messages which may be against what you, as an artist, want to communicate. It's a bit of a strained relationship. I don't know what I can say about the future of it, but the arts have always been a vital part of society. So, there should be that connection. As an organisation based in Berlin, we haven't made as active an effort as we should to reach out to the embassies. But it also has to do with where we see more opportunities as a collective. So, we tend to gravitate towards non-governmental organisations.

TC: Today, soon after this, I will be meeting with Chirikure Chirikure who is in Germany for the Frankfurt Book Fair. Which brings me to the next question: Germany has hosted many great Zimbabwean artists and African artists in general. For instance, the African Literature Festival in Berlin has hosted the likes of Emmanuel Sigauke, Ben Okri, NoVuyo Rosa Tshuma, Chirikure Chirikure, Zukiswa Wanner and the like. Do you see Isusu Ffena hosting such big names in the future? One of the coodinators in your collective is from Uganda. I am thinking of someone like Stella Nyanzi here for instance, who is here as a Pen fellow, but also in some kind of exile from Museveni.

MC: We've actually worked with Tsitsi Dangarembga. We hosted an online event in 2020 in which we were exploring colonial legacies in tourism.

TC: Let me interrupt you there. I think that aspect you are talking about is one of the most iconic passages in *This Mournable Body*. I really liked the way she tackled it.

MC: Yes, we talked about that and about *This Mournable Body*. So I can say we have had the opportunity to work with some big names. But to be honest, the greatest hurdle for us is that big names require big money. I really feel that it is really fair for artists to make certain demands for appearances. Art pays. So, the onus is on us to grow to such a level as to attract big funding and big artists. But, to tell you the truth, as a collective, we are excited about the idea of bringing in new artists. Part of our charm is working with artists who are not as widely known as, say, Tsitsi Dangarembga. Remember how exciting your session with Tanatsei Gumbura was? So many people came and many of them were hearing about you for the first time but they were blown away. So, while we are working on widening our reputation to attract big names, I want to say that what we are doing now is equally important. We are casting the spotlight on artists that wouldn't otherwise have managed to reach certain audiences here in Berlin. So there is value in all the artists we bring in. At the end of the day, it's not really about the name, but about the type of work the artist is bringing.

TC: Speaking of my session with Tanatsei Gambura, she couldn't be physically present in Berlin, but we still managed to have a seamless event over Zoom. Do you think COVID-19 has also opened possibilities for collaborations with various artists from all over the world, something that could have been difficult in the pre-covid-19 era where face-to-face interaction was the norm?

MC: Tanatsei was not the only artist who couldn't come. We had Wandy Pascal, Simba Mafundikwa and Wonai Hauperi who couldn't be present. So, yea, Covid-19 has opened our minds. These possibilities are not being discovered now; Zoom and Skype have always been there before Covid-19, but our minds were not open to the possibilities of holding events online. We didn't think of these online apps as spaces that can allow exciting collaborations and the holding of events. But as Isusu Ffena, we thrive on creating a sense of community. We believe that it is easier to create that feeling in face-to-face interaction than online. But as you know, we couldn't hold our festival in 2021 because of COVID-19 restrictions, but we still managed to hold lots of events. It was heartwarming to see, under those conditions of lockdown, someone joining from Hong Kong, Tanzania, and so on. So we had a community that went beyond the borders of Germany.

TC: From what I have seen, the future is brighter, the possibilities are wider. I think beyond just Zimbabweans in Berlin, Isusu Ffena has the potential to become a Europe-wide festival. I recently attended a Zimbabwean funeral in Belgium. I met Zimbabweans from the UK, Spain, Portugal, Netherlands, Germany, Belgium and so on, who had come to bid farewell to one of their own. It opened my eyes to the existence of a Zimbabwean community that transcends the borders of a specific European country. I think festivals like the Isusu Ffena can catalyse such Europe-wide collaborations between Zimbabweans. My last question, then, is: Do you see Isusu Ffena expanding to that level?

MC: The big dream of Isusu Ffena is actually to have a moving festival. The four of us who are Zimbabwean were born and raised in Harare. One of our big sources of inspiration is HIFA which is no longer being held in that form anymore. So we imagine ourselves having something that big all over Europe. Imagine Isusu Ffena in Brussels, Isusu Ffena in Amsterdam and so on.

TC: That would be awesome! Well, thank you, Mareika for this stimulating conversation. I wish you and the Isusu Ffena family all the best. I think you are poised for something great, especially from what I have seen.

MC: Thank you, Tanaka, and thank you for honouring our inivitation.

TC: I should actually be thanking you. Meeting people from diverse backgrounds and reading and talking about my poetry was one of the highlights of 2022 for me. I am sure I will be at the 2023 Festival.

MC: I am actually inviting you in advance.

TC: For your flu, if you were in Zimbabwe my grandmother would be doting on you with zumbani leaves.

MC: I am actually drinking a zumbani concoction right now. I brought some from Zimbabwe

We laughed uproariously like Zimbabweans and would have slapped each other's palms were it not for the limitations of ZOOM.

Interview of Tendai Rinos Mwanaka music album, Logbook Written by a Drifter

Dizzy Storms

*H*ow did you get started in music? Professionally it was in 2014 when I shortchanged my sister of her Mbira instrument and started learning how to play it. But I have always been interested in music from when I was little. I remember I made the school choir in grade 2, and I have been in several choirs including church choirs, where I would lead the choirs too.

What are your inspirations or influences?
African music, songs we grew up singing, songs I sang at the church, songs from my Shona culture, and western music in the form of RNB, pop, Rock and opera classics. I am inspired by the beauty and uniqueness of music and sound. Yes I love good lyrics but I think what really inspires me about music is the music, it's inside stories, conventions, music varieties, experimentation etc... I am a multidisciplinary artist, with literary, Visual and musical strands of my career all off the base. So I am always interested in finding links between these fields, and in music I have done that by combining the literary aspects in the form of the poetic genre with music... because of my African experience there is a certain formless and transcendence that my music has, and the western music sometimes corals it through its insistence on structure and form. In my Lockdown journal, day 10: I wrote, "literature makes me burrow inside the suffocating walls until I find a small ledge in the walls where I can hide and avoid being crushed by the walls. Visual art left me for 3 weeks now, may hands have no eyes to see, it's of no use now because visual art would crush the walls to debris, to reconstruct them. So I am left with musical art to maintain space around me and push the walls without breaking them. We are supposed to stay indoors! I need the walls to keep me

focused, to commute with this imprisonment." Thus music, like in those images of the Italians standing on their balconies in Rome and belting songs and sorrow, trying to deal with mounting deaths of covid 19, music helps me deal with life threatening situation. So music is my last stand, the thing that holds everything together.

What advice will you give aspiring performers?

Be open to the sounds, experiment, be patient, work harder and keep trying even if it doesn't make sense now

How do you set yourself apart from other bands or singers?

As I noted I am interested in the music more than the lyrics and I work from my culture and mix it with western influences, thus my sounds are always unique. I use Mbira and Marimba to compose the melodies of songs such that the African melodies cannot be overshadowed by the western elements I would add through the keyboards, there is asymmetrical laying between the two influences to create a poetic sound. So my music could be interpreted as literature music

Any new gigs or albums in the future

Yes I recently released my first album of music and poetry. The music is Marimba inspired, with all sorts of keyboard including among others, Cello, Violin, Horns, Flute, Harp, Bells, sticks etc. it's a 9 track album entitled *Logbook Written by a Drifter* (title borrowed from my collection of poetry with same title, and most of the lyrics are poems from this collection), a few songs were recently published by University of Texas Austin, Apricity here: https://apricitymagazine.com/portfolio/tendai-rinos-mwanaka-compositions/ and the rest are on my soundcloud here: https://soundcloud.com/tendai-rinos-mwanaka

The Dust is the Theory
Tendai Rinos Mwanaka

We were full of beef, always looking for attention, behaving like utter freaks. My closest friend who wasn't a close relative was David Mukonomushava. I heard he died a few years ago. Growing old is becoming a witness on how everything you have valued starts disappearing until you wonder, is this all you were ever meant to do in life. Being a witness, but who would witness you if you overstayed everyone, when death was exhausted of death, who would console you? Of course I was much more close to my cousin, Fungai, whom I shared the same class with from Grade six onwards, we also sat on the same benches in form 1 and 2. With David we were inseparable for some time, at the height of my hunt for mischief. Every Friday we always stayed behind doing punishment for infractions we had incurred during the week. We were anti-establishment to the hilt. If the school introduces any rule which was an infraction to our independence and freedom, we would fight it head on. There is a time the school introduced English speaking to improve English understanding, they said. I think Mr. Chibvuri was behind it, as he was the acting head waiting for our substantial headmaster, Mr Nyamandwe, who was on leave after finishing his tenure at his previous school, St Davids Bonda, waiting to take over at Nyatate.

So they had created small stripes of papers written, "I am a Shona Speaker". Imagine the irony of having to admit to talking in your language as an infraction. Being a Shona speaker was punishable now, yet you are actually a Shona person. A drop of water had become guilty of flooding. Imagine asking an English man to be punished for being an English speaker at school. Here is what would happen, the class monitors, prefects and head boy and head girl would start with these slips of papers. They would give them to the next student they find speaking Shona. That student is supposed to give it to the next student, next student… until the last student who had those slips by Friday afternoon would be asked to stay behind for punishment and or tell the prefects who had passed the paper to them, until the whole lineage of Shona speakers that week were booked for punishment. It felt like punishing your ancestors for birthing you. And by that first Friday we had collected most of the slips and we refused to tell the prefects where we had got them. We never spoke English and we collected most of the slips and never passed them off to the next student as was the rule. It took us a few weeks to disrupt this and hoard all the slips every time they were issued, and every Friday afternoon we stayed behind doing punishment for the whole school. That was a given for us, as we broke many other rules. At one time, midyear form 2, I missed a technical drawing exam doing punishment but the teacher, who was also the headmaster, Makwaza, gave me a zero on the report card, and yet I still comfortably made the top 5 in that class. We were insufferably mischievous such that the school made sure we were never invited to any functions or events because we were sure to create drama

There is this time a local teacher died and the school closed and the whole student body went to the funeral. We were told by the headmaster, Mr Makwaza, to stay at school, afraid we will create drama at the funeral. But as long as you didn't tie us down we refused to graze where were not tied down, I am just paraphrasing the Shona proverb here, "a goat grazes around the place it is tied down on". There was no way we were going to respect any instruction. So we waited for an hour and followed the students to the residence of this teacher who had recently departed. My mother said when she saw me she hid, and when the students saw us some started laughing, giggling, gawking … knowing we were up for it.

We started crying in high pitched voices, crying like hell had broken loose and we were squirming from the hot hell, like utter crazies, mourning this teacher. We would throw ourselves on the ground, keening and belting another glossolalia. One would have thought we were moved by this death if you were not privy to our work. We hated this teacher from our years at the primary school where the teacher taught for years of my primary school years. That teacher was a fucker of the first order. I remember how on the first day of the school, my little sister was wacked by the backhand of this teacher for messing up the school's march from Assembly. We were trained like soldiers at a barrack. You wouldn't just amble away from the assembly like the kids do nowadays. The first class, grade 1 A, then Grade 1 B, then Grade 1 C, grade 2 A, Grade 2 B, Grade 2 C….that was the system we had to follow. Not only will you be marching, stomping your feet down like a soldier, we would also be singing songs, to the drum we would mock sing to later on as saying, *gandatiganda mwana ane manyoka, gandatiganda mwana ane manyoka* would be belted, and you have to be swinging your hands twice upwards, and once downwards, your legs in synchronicity to the beat and the pace of the march as you moved in one single file from the assembly, class after class, using the alphabetical spellings of your surnames in that class. I don't think we had a surname that started with letter A in Shona, so the Bores, Binungus, Bangojena, The Chikwandingwas, Chibvuris…were up there ahead in the lines, and of course the Mwanakas were in the middle tail end of the lines.

My little sister had stumbled trying to climb the over 2 metres high steps to the grade 1 class, tumbling down taking a number of kids down with her. Only for her to tumble down again as the teacher's backhand wacked her to the ground. First day at school, a little six year old is expected to be drilled and be a perfect soldier. This teacher was a cruel disciplinarian.

And so when the head boy realized we were upto our usual tricks, a Simon Huna, who was the head boy and the other older form 4 guys grabbed us by our feet and hands, shutting our mouths and carried us off the funeral. We didn't care. We had made our point. Later, in our form 4, we lost another teacher we loved, who was my cousin, Bizzet Mapfurira. It gutted me. Even though I had performed at the primary school teacher's funeral when he died, this time I learned that loss is personal. Even though my cousin, when he was our accounting teacher, was strict on me and would beat me up if I misbehaved, his death broke something in me

He was gunned down by the police in Harare where he was finishing off his studies at Harare polytechnic, a few months after he had married his long time sweetheart. With the death of my grandmother when in form 2, I realized death stalked everything that I thought was permanent. Bit by bit loosing people I knew taught me I had to make the best out of this now. Earth was only a school, and dust was the only theory we had to learn and relearn, and relearn for a lifetime of it...

USED, ABUSED and REFUSED, Part Three

The plight of Zimbabwe's National Liberation War Veterans, 45 years on

Killian Mwanaka (aka Cde Ducas Fambai)

Zimbabwe, the sick-man of the corrupt world

Zimbabwe is a nation continuously bleeding to death because of corruption. Corruption has pervaded in all the fabric of Zimbabwe's social strata. You have to pay money to someone in the Passport Office to have your documents processed. A student must pay the headmaster of a school to secure a vacancy for education. You have to pay someone money to show you where Munhumutapa Building is. Government contracts are awarded to family and friends without going to tender. The list of corrupt activities in Zimbabwe is long.

The Chinese and other nationals corruptly pay some officials in party and government to secure mining rights and other national resources. The plunder of Zimbabwe's national resources by foreign nationals, especially the Chinese, is hurting our nation's economy. As a result of this, our mineral resources have been scooped and sent away to develop other countries. It is known that the Chinese have flattened whole hills using strong dynamites when they smell gold or other minerals underneath. Hills in Boterekwa, in Shurugwi, are a case in point. The hills have been levelled to the ground as the Chinese plunderers search for gold and other minerals on our land.

To add salt to the wound, the Chinese are known to abuse and insult Zimbabweans in their work-places. They spit them in their faces and call them 'monkeys' as they toil in mines and other factories. The

216

Chinese are allowed to carry guns and are even known to shoot Zimbabweans. Ask yourself this question, can a Zimbabwean go to China and do what the Chinese are doing to us in Zimbabwe? What really is the problem with Zimbabwe? It is its leadership – Period! Our leadership is disgustingly sickening; sickening to the core!

What our government and party officials don't seem to understand is that minerals don't grow; once they are dug out from the ground, they are irreplaceable. When the Chinese finish with us and go back to their country, we will be left with nothing, but a scarred land with dongas and deep gullies.

Is the President of the country, Mnangagwa, not aware of this? What deal did he strike with the Chinese to let them plunder our country and dehumanise our people at will? The Chinese's plunder of our natural resources is an extension of their desire to scoop all natural recourses across the African continent. The Chinese are causing mining havoc in the DRC, Zambia, Tanzania, everywhere in Africa. They have emerged as a vicious new economic exploiter.

As national liberation war veterans, what are we doing about corruption? What are we doing about the Chinese's continued plunder of our mineral resources? Standing and staring! It is time, we get into the streets. We must march along the streets of our cities and towns with placards screaming, 'Pasi ne'corruption!' 'Corruption has killed our country!' 'Corrupt officials are traitors of the revolution!' 'Corrupt officials must go to jail!' 'Enough of Chinese mineral plunder!' 'Chinese go back home!'

When we do this, the 'povo' will rally behind us. They will see us as true revolutionaries. With the 'povo', we can go all the way and kick out this fuckin' regime that has impoverished Zimbabweans and instilled fear amongst our people.

Ma'comrades' it is time we side with the 'povo'. If we keep supporting this rotten Mnangagwa regime, history will not absolve us. Cases of corruption by government and party officials are reported by the independent newspapers in Zimbabwe almost on a daily basis. And what is our response as national liberation war veterans? We spring to the defence of the party and government thieves with statements like, "This is not true. These reports are manufactured by people who hate ZANU-PF." Really! What is wrong with us ma'comrades? We must stop supporting these people who are looting our national wealth. We must stop protecting them. We must stop being used by them.

What is surprising with us is that when Mnangagwa appears in our midst, instead of telling him 'Piss off! You thief', we howl, 'chef, chef' leaking his boots. Are we not aware that this is the NUMBER ONE THIEF in Zimbabwe. Are we not aware that this is the man who is causing misery to all Zimbabweans? Are we not aware that this is the man who has staffed most strategic government and military institutions with his sons and clans-men? Are we not aware that this is the culprit who does not want increment of our welfare benefits, and that he is the LEADER OF CORRUPTION in Zimbabwe? And when he says, "Indai mundo ponda mhandu dzeZANU-PF!' we break Usain Bolt's hundred-meter record, chasing and killing members of the opposition.

Corruption in Zimbabwe is nauseatingly disgusting. Take this scenario; I am a businessman in London. My company, 'Mwanaka Fresh Farm Shop', (MFFF), imports products that include drinks (Mazowe, fizzy drinks …), ma'things', nyimo, nzungu, mbambaira …for the Zimbabwean and Afro-Caribbean community in the UK.

On this day, I am in Harare at a company… (name withheld) with US$20,000 in my purse intending to buy a large quantity of Mazoe drinks (Orange, Cream Soda, Raspberry, Peach and Blackberry). I understand some of the drinks produced by this company are for 'export market' and are cheaper. And when I get into the Sales Department, I ask to buy the drinks and specify the types and quantity I want to buy.

The gentleman seating in a chair (presumably the Sales Manager) takes his calculator and does a quick calculation. "US$15,000!" he says and looks at me with a flashy smile. "Do you have the money to pay?"

"Oh yes, I do," I calmly say, expecting to go ahead with the purchase of the drinks.

"Mudhara mune marika imi," he says looking at me with renewed interest.

"Kungobatanidza-batanidza kuti zvifambe, you know," I tersely answer.

"You know mudhara, we are not allowed to sell even half of the quantity you want. We have a restriction of quantity to sell." After a pause and with a firm voice emitting a fetid smell of corruption he continues, "But, mukangondidonhedzera kaTwo chete, zvinhu zvese zvinofamba." ("But, if you just give me Two.")

That's when I realise, he wants me to give him US$200.00 chioko muhomwe (palm greasing money.) At this stark realisation, I storm out of his office and go to Muhamed Musa Wholesalers where I buy my drinks untroubled.

The above is petty corruption in comparison to billions of dollars in gold, diamonds, lithium and other precious minerals being siphoned from Zimbabwe through corrupt deals.

It is known that Zimbabwe has over 40 different types of minerals that include rare earth minerals. Rare earth minerals that Zimbabwe is known to have include, niobium, strontium, titanium, and zirconium. Google says, 'The predominant minerals (in Zimbabwe) include platinum group of metals (PGM), chrome, gold, coal and diamonds. The country boasts the second-largest platinum deposits and high-grade chromium ores in the world, with approximately 2.8 billion tons of chromium ore.' Google, 2 January 2025.

But there is virtually nothing to show (in economic development) for Zimbabwe's vast mineral resources.

Gas and oil have been reportedly discovered in Muzarabani. This discovery will come to naught in economic terms for our nation, just like the plunder of Chiadzwa diamonds that left only deep scars to our environment.

If all Zimbabwe's minerals were well-managed, coupled with tobacco and cotton and other agricultural produce from the land and tourism, our country should be able to stand head and shoulders above many African and European nations in terms of development.

Ask yourself, why countries like Norway, Sweden, Finland, Denmark and Korea are managing their economies efficiently and successfully with only timber and fisheries and a few minerals while Zimbabwe is languishing in poverty with abundant natural resources? The answer is in leadership. 'Africa has everything but leaders,' is a common agreeable and indisputable fact. Mobutu plundered DRC and the current Tshisekedi leadership is mired in corruption. Yoweri Museveni has ruled Uganda as his fiefdom installing his relatives to the highest offices in the country. Teodoro Obiang Nguema Mbasogo, Equatorial Guinea President since 1982 has plundered the country's resources unquestioned. The list goes on and on. And Zimbabwe!

We (national liberation war veterans) have gone into the streets with placards requesting increment of our pension money, but government has remained mum to our demands. It (government) has even sent police and soldiers to beat and arrest us when we make our legitimate demands. Why does government not pay attention to our demands for increment of our pension funds? The answer is government has no money. Government is broke. But money is there; plenty of it; billions if not trillions of dollars, in mineral and other resources. But the money is in the hands of a few, mainly those who have managed and are managing to acquire it corruptly. They build mansions with it and siphon billions of it to off-shore accounts. Money is in the hands of Chivayos and company who go about buying vehicles for the Zimbabwean elite (to garner cheap popularity) and forget that

Parirenyatwa, Harare and other hospitals need X-rays machines, beds and ambulances to function.

The Zimbabwean elite are vying to be on the Forbes' rich list while the 'povo' find it difficult to put bread on their table.

And, to cover their corrupt trails, they tell the nation that Zimbabwe is languishing in poverty due to sanctions imposed by the western countries. What a subterfuge! You know what ma'comrades', Cuba, an island surrounded by the Atlantic Ocean, with no mineral resources to talk of, has survived the onslaught of American sanctions but has produced doctors and other medical staff and soldiers to help other countries in need. A case in point is Cuba's intervention to assist Angola's MPLA (Movemento Popular de Libertacao de Angola) fighting Jonas Savimbi's South African-backed UNITA (Uniao National para a Independencia Total de Angola) in a war fought in Cuito Cuanavale between Decemeber 1987 and March 1988, that ended with the ignominious defeat of the apartheid South African forces. Cuba has stood head and shoulders above USA sanctions attack. Why should Zimbabwe talk of sanctions when all Africa, the eastern world (India, China, Japan etc.) and South America (Brazil, Argentine, Mexico …) are there to trade with. What we know for certain is that if sanctions are lifted and lines of credit are opened, and millions of dollars start pouring into the country from the World Bank, IMF and other international money-lending institutions, they (the usual looters) will clean the banks empty, and all the money will never be accounted for. This money (from the World Bank, IMF and other international money-lending institutions) that Zimbabwe needs, is a miniscule compared to the money our minerals are generating but siphoned out of the country corruptly. The mention of 'sanctions' is only a smokescreen for looting and nothing else

Corruption in Zimbabwe has hung our country on the precipice of economic decay.

It's not true that Zimbabwe is denied trade with the UK because of sanctions. Recently, I saw packs of granadillas labelled 'product of Zimbabwe' in Sainsbury's supermarket. How would this agricultural product from Zimbabwe find its way to the UK supermarket's shelf if UK had sanctions imposed on Zimbabwe. Tesco's, Sainsbury's, Aldi's and many other supermarkets in the UK are starved of vegetables. The UK will not say, 'No!' to our organic cabbages, peas, cucumbers, fruit etc. because they don't have them. But how would these products come to the UK when Zimbabwe does not have air freight?

While President Mnangagwa's mantra is, "Zimbabwe is open for business," how many business-people will be 'open' to invest in a country so rampant with corruption.? As corruption rages on unchecked, it is apparent that some foreign investors will continue to desist investing in Zimbabwe, returning to their countries with millions of dollars that could have benefitted our country's economy and curb unemployment. As national liberation war veterans, it is our duty to stand against the tide of corruption and help stop it.

Gwara remusangano

I have heard many times many of us (national liberation war veterans) uttering this statement, 'Macomrades, tinofanirwa kuchengetedza gwara remusangano." Literally translated this means, "Comrades, we must guard the party's ideology'. The question is, "What is the party's ideology we are talking about?' 'What is gwara remusangano?' My assertion is that the party has its leaders and those leaders must, first and foremost, be the guardians of the party's ideology. They must be the spearheads of the party's ideology.

The behavioural pattern of ZANU-PF and government officials is that they are looters, thieves and robbers. They have neglected hospitals, roads and schools. They have stopped construction of factories which would produce products for domestic consumption and export and create employment. They are selfish. They are nepotists. They are tribalists. They are hedonists. They are murderers. All these characteristics embody ZANU-PF officials' behaviour which can rightly be called its ideology. So, next time fellow comrades, when you say, 'gwara remusangano', remember that you are talking of these characteristics.

What is surprising with our party and government officials is that, with the monies they loot, they go on holidays abroad to astonishingly wonderfully developed places like Dubai, Hong Kong and Miami. We expect that when they come back home, they would have copied what they would have seen in these holiday destinations and implement them in their own country. No. So, really, what do we call these people? Madofo chaiwo asingagone nekucopa. Madofo anongogona kuba chete. Surely, this is laughable.

I invite national liberation war veterans to proffer their view of 'gwara remusangaro' that differs from my observation.

In the same vein as the absence of ideology in ZANU-PF, it is surprising that we call the party, 'revolutionary party'. Why do we call ZANU-PF a 'revolutionary party'? My assertion is that ZANU-PF is not a revolutionary party. A revolutionary party follows a revolutionary ideology that transforms the lives of the people. A revolutionary party looks after the welfare of its people. A revolutionary party looks after the welfare of the people (national liberation war veterans) who put it into power. A revolutionary party develops the nation - hospitals, roads, provision of water, education – in all aspects of the nation's sphere. Is ZANU-PF doing all these? No, it's not! So, ZANU-PF is not a revolutionary party. It is something else. The antithesis of 'a revolutionary party' is a 'reactionary party'. So, in essence, ZANU-PF is a reactionary party. ZANU-PF is only a revolutionary party in rhetoric.

Zvivanhu zviya

Our situation as national liberation war veterans is a predicament, indeed, an irony of unimaginable proportions. While our 'chefs' don't like us, the Zimbabwean population don't like us either; they hate us actually. Idiomatically speaking, we are caught between a rock and a hard place. Take this scenario of a few years ago: I am in London, and I phone my friend in Harare intending to ascertain the state of the situation in my country.

"How are you and everyone else in Harare?" I start the conversation.

"Kuri right hako but zvivanhu zviya zviri mustreet," my friend says. My friend works in the UK but had just gone back to 'sort out things' in Zimbabwe.

225

"What do you mean 'zvivanhu zviya zviri mustreet'? I ask.

"Zviri kudemonstrator for more pension money," he says.

"You mean the teachers?"

"No, not the teachers, Bro. I mean izvi zvakarwa hondo. Izvi zvakauraya vanhu izvi."

That's when I realise, he is talking of the national liberation war veterans. They were in the streets demonstrating for more pension money, which issue eventually escalated with the national liberation war veterans suing the state. The case is still pending in the courts. The national liberation war veterans suing the state! Isn't this embarrassing? Isn't this akin to a child suing his/her father?

My friend does not know I am also a national liberation war veteran. He doesn't know I am part of the people he is calling, 'izvi zvakarwa hondo', I never disclose my identity to him, so he continues speaking at will.

"You know what, I hate these guys. I hate them with a passion," he says.

"But isn't it them who fought for the independence of our country?" I say, still not revealing my identity.

"They may have fought for our independence, but they are idiots Bro."

"Why do you call them idiots when we should call them heroes for what they did for our country – liberating us from colonial bondage?"

"Are you not aware Bro, that these guys are propping up this fuckin' Mnangagwa regime that has made life miserable for all Zimbabweans? And look what they are, mamvenve evanhu, mamvemve chaiwo. They keep saying, "Takasunungura nyika, takasunungura nyika, ngavadzorere nyika yacho kwayakanga yakasungirirwa.""

I realise I am speaking with someone who has an entrenched hatred for national liberation war veterans, whose mind is a complete departure from patriotism. I am flabbergasted. I am dismayed. I am disgusted. I am angry. However, despite my overwhelming sense of revulsion from the interactive discussion with my friend, I realise that this is an irrefutable epitome of what some Zimbabweans, if not most of them, view us national liberation war veterans.

Mmap Nonfiction and Academic books

If you have enjoyed *Zimbolicious 10th Anniversary Anthology: New and Collected Non-fictions* consider these other fine **Mmap Nonfiction and Academic books** from *Mwanaka Media and Publishing:*

Cultural Hybridity and Fixity by Andrew Nyongesa
Tintinnabulation of Literary Theory by Andrew Nyongesa
South Africa and United Nations Peacekeeping Offensive Operations by Antonio Garcia
A Case of Love and Hate by Chenjerai Mhondera
A Cat and Mouse Affair by Bruno Shora
The Scholarship Girl by Abigail George
The Gods Sleep Through It All by Wonder Guchu
PHENOMENOLOGY OF DECOLONIZING THE UNIVERSITY: Essays in the Contemporary Thoughts of Afrikology by Zvikomborero Kapuya
Africanization and Americanization Anthology Volume 1, Searching for Interracial, Interstitial, Intersectional and Interstates Meeting Spaces, Africa Vs North America by Tendai R Mwanaka
Africa, UK and Ireland: Writing Politics and Knowledge Production Vol 1 by Tendai R Mwanaka
Writing Language, Culture and Development, Africa Vs Asia Vol 1 by Tendai R Mwanaka, Wanjohi wa Makokha and Upal Deb
Zimbolicious: An Anthology of Zimbabwean Literature and Arts, Vol 3 by Tendai Mwanaka
Drawing Without Licence by Tendai R Mwanaka
Writing Grandmothers/ Escribiendo sobre nuestras raíces: Africa Vs Latin America Vol 2 by Tendai R Mwanaka and Felix Rodriguez

Nationalism: (Mis)Understanding Donald Trump's Capitalism, Racism, Global Politics, International Trade and Media Wars, Africa Vs North America Vol 2 by Tendai R Mwanaka

It Is Not About Me: Diaries 2010-2011 by Tendai Rinos Mwanaka

Chitungwiza Mushamukuru: An Anthology from Zimbabwe's Biggest Ghetto Town by Tendai Rinos Mwanaka

The Day and the Dweller: A Study of the Emerald Tablets by Jonathan Thompson

Zimbolicious Anthology Vol 4: An Anthology of Zimbabwean Literature and Arts by Tendai Rinos Mwanaka and Jabulani Mzinyathi

Parks and Recreation by Abigail George

FAMILY LAW AND POLITICS WITH BIOLOGY AND ROYALTY IN AFRICA AND NORTH AMERICA by Peter Ateh-Afec Fossungu

Writing Robotics, Africa Vs Asia, Vol 2 by Tendai Rinos Mwanaka

Zimbolicious Anthology Vol 5: An Anthology of Zimbabwean Literature and Arts by Tendai R. Mwanaka

Love Notes: Everything is Love, An Anthology of Indigenous Languages of Africa and East Europe by Tendai R Mwanaka

Zimbolicious Anthology Vol 6: An Anthology of Zimbabwean Literature and Arts by Tendai R. Mwanaka and Chenjerai Mhondera

BATTLING LANGUAGE RIGHTS GOVERNANCE IN AFRICA: SWISSELGIANISM, UBACKISM, AND THE AMBAZONIA-CAMEROUN WAR by Peter Ateh-Afec Fossungu

Otherness and Pathology: The Fragmented Self and Madness in Contemporary African Fiction by Andrew Nyongesa

Zimbabwe: The Urgency of Now by Tendai Rinos Mwanaka

Zimbabwe: The Blame Game, Recollected essays and Non-fictions by Tendai Rinos Mwanaka

The Trick is to Keep Breathing: Covid 19 Stories From African and North American Writers, Vol 3 by Tendai Rinos Mwanaka

Recentring Mother Earth by Andrew Nyongesa

Zimbabwe: Beyond Robert Mugabe by Tendai Rinos Mwanaka

Language, Thought, Art and Existence: New and Recollected Essays and Non Fictions by Tendai Rinos Mwanaka

Experimental Writing, Africa Vs Latin America Vol 1 by Tendai Rinos Mwanaka and Ricardo Felix Rodriguez

Fixing Earth Anthology: An anthology of Africa, UK and Ireland Writers, Vol 2 by Tendai Rinos Mwanaka

Africa Must Deal with Blats for Its True Decolonisation: Unclothed Truth about Internalised Internal Colonialism by Nkwazi N. Mhango

ROYAL BURIAL AND ENTHRONEMENT IN AMBAZONIA: INTERROGATING THE RELEVANCE OF POSTCOLONIAL EDUCATION IN AFRICA by Peter Ateh-Afec Fossungu

SCHOOL BASED HIV EDUCATION AFFECTING GIRLS IN SELECTED COUNTRIES IN SUB SAHARAN AFRICA by Ivainesu Charmaine Musa

HIV AND AIDS IN ZIMBABWE: A REVIEW ON THE RELATIONSHIP BETWEEN PERCEPTION OF MASCULINITY AMONGST UNMARRIED YOUNG MEN AND THEIR SEXUAL BEHAVIORS by Lucas Kudakwashe Muvhiringi

AFRICA'S CONTEMPORARY FOOD INSECURITY: SELF-INFLICTED WOUNDS THROUGH MODERN VENI VIDI VICI AND LAND GRABBING by Nkwazi Mhango

I Can't Breathe and other Essays by Zvikomborero Kapuya

Ayabacholization Classroom In My Life: The Longest Shortcut To University Education by Peter Ateh-Afec Fossungu

Gathering Evidence by Tendai Rinos Mwanaka

Best New African poets 10th anniversary: Interviews and Reviews by Tendai Rinos Mwanaka

In the footsteps of a Bipolar Life by Ambrose Cato George and Abigail George

No Business Like Love Business by Peter Atec-Afec Fossungu

RE-ENGINEERING UNDER-EXPLORED RENEWABLE ENERGY by Blessing Barnet Chiniko

Manifestations of trauma in the post-2000 Zimbabwean Literature by Nyarai Maria Kanyemba

Donald Trump's Second Coming: Is Democracy, Dead, Dying or Alive by Tendai Rinos Mwanaka

HISTORY IN HISTORY OF AMBAZONIA RESISTENCE by Peter Afec-Ateh Fossungu

Upcoming books

https://facebook.com/MwanakaMediaAndPublishing